Veronica Cane

For more information please contact Veronica Cane directly www.VeronicaCane.com.

ISBN-13: 978-1512257281
ISBN-10: 1512257281

WARNING

While this book does not contain any actual photos or visual depictions of nudity, due to the nature of the content within the pages of this book, you should be 18 years of age or older to read any further. This book deals specifically with concepts of adult sexual encounters that may or may not be appropriate for you. This book deals with fantasy and fetish including all sorts of BDSM and bondage themes. If you are easily offended by unusual or unique sexual circumstances, this probably isn't the book for you.

Table of Contents

Chapter 1

Growing up, I didn't have the luxury of believing in little girl fairy tales. I didn't dream that Prince Charming would one day come and take me away. I knew life for what it was, a cold and harsh place where daddies went away and mommies worked two and sometimes three jobs to try and support their children. And even then, that wasn't a guarantee that food would always be on the table.

My mother did the best she could, but with five children, it wasn't easy on her. Even when I got old enough to take on part time work, we all still struggled just to survive.

Two days after my seventeenth birthday, my mother died after a long bout with pneumonia. My elder brother Charlie could only afford to keep one of us and since I was the only one old enough to work, he chose me. The younger children were sent off to foster homes. A few months later, Charlie got into a car wreck and he died too. So I was officially on my own.

Although I graduated high school, I couldn't exactly afford to go to college, so I took any job I could. Anyone that would hire someone without any real skills or work experience. One day, while working for a temp agency, the girl at the front desk suggested I come in and hone my computer skills. She said that if I could improve them, she would be able to place me in higher paying jobs. I spent every free minute I could in their office practicing anything and everything they could teach me.

Eventually I was able to pass the skills test to become an entry level secretary. Some people might laugh or turn their nose up at such a job, but it was the best job I ever had and a huge step up from waitressing or the retail sales gigs I normally got. I felt like I had a career, or at least the start of one.

The temp agency kept me pretty busy, always placing me in new jobs, as soon as my last assignment was over. Finally, one day I got the call for a long term placement at one of those big fancy downtown law firms. The pay was fantastic and if I did well, I had the opportunity for a permanent job with the company, after six months. And that would include benefits like health insurance, paid vacations and retirement. It was a dream come true and I knew I would do whatever it took to make these people love me so I could have that permanent position with the company.

Unfortunately, I found out rather quickly that this law firm hired so many people from the temp agency so that they could always keep fresh meat coming in. The boss was a total and complete pervert and used the temp agency more like a dating service. The girls that would sleep with him got to stay, the ones who didn't put out, found themselves replaced.

I lasted only three weeks. But that was just long enough to figure out the kind of skills a law firm was looking for in their clerical staff. I knew one day another position like that would come available and I wanted to be ready.

A year later that call did come and by then I was a pro at the computer and with the software they used.

This law firm, Ashworth and Kent specialized in International law and had offices around the globe. Their main office was in London and many of the senior partners were British. I had landed the job as the personal assistant to one of the partners, Julian Moretti.

On the long elevator ride up to the thirty-third floor, I gave myself a pep talk. "You can do this. He's just like anyone else. Don't be nervous. He's not going to bite you. He's no different than anyone else. Even if he does happen to be rich. His money doesn't matter. He's still a normal guy."

My stomach was in knots. I'd never met anyone like Julian Moretti before and now I was going to be working for him, interacting with him day in and day out. He was a powerful man, a legal genius, who was said to be able to take even the worst cases and somehow win them.

I caught sight of myself in the oversized mirrors. I was having a great hair day and was sure that was a sign that today was going to go well. I was glad to be alone in the elevator so that others wouldn't see me looking at myself and admiring how my long blonde hair fell in soft waves, framing my perfectly made up face. That would be rather embarrassing.

Normally I didn't like to trade off of my looks, but still I couldn't help it if they gave me an advantage at times. I only hoped that today of all days, it worked towards my benefit. I needed everything I could get. I'd heard that Julian Moretti could be rather intimidating. Maybe if he thought I was pretty, he would go easier on me -- it was my first day after all.

I still couldn't believe I was hired as the executive assistant to Julian Moretti at Ashworth and Kent no less. They employed thousands of people all over the globe. Finally I had a job with actual opportunity for growth.

I never dreamed that I would be so lucky to land such a great paying job in my entire life. Okay sure I dreamed that I would get a job like this, but I never thought that dream would be a reality. There were no doubt hundreds of people who applied for the position and yet somehow, after three interviews, a skills test and a background check, I got the job.

And now here I am, on the first day, and I couldn't figure out whatever made me think I could handle the job of working for such an important man.

The elevator sounding my arrival snapped me to. I took several deep breaths. Reminding myself that I could do this.

The doors opened up to a massive lobby with a round desk front in center. Behind the desk was an older woman, probably in her late forties with her hair in a tight bun on top of her head and a big smile plastered on her face.

Two white marble columns flanked the elevator doors which matched the white and black marble floors of the lobby. In the corner there was a seating area with black leather furniture with a matching modern designed table and lamp. The room felt cold and lifeless, even with the exquisite paintings that hung on the wall that would normally give a room a depth of warmth. The room still just felt like a museum. On the other side of the room there was a floor-to-ceiling window with a view of the Houston skyline. It was a stunning view.

I felt increasingly inadequate as I stepped up to the desk in my second hand business-suit and borrowed Christian Louboutin heels.

"Can I help you?" The woman asked as I stood self-consciously before her.

"Yes I'm Elizabeth Seabrook, Mr. Moretti's new assistant."

The woman pushed a button and spoke into her headset. "Mr. Moretti, I have Elizabeth Seabrook here, who says she's your new assistant."

She paused for a few moments. "Okay. Yes sir."

She pushed the button again, disconnecting the call and then turned back to me. "Mr. Moretti said to take a seat. He'll send someone to get you shortly."

The woman pointed towards the black leather couches in the corner of the room. She didn't give me another glance as she turned back to her computer.

Before I had a chance to even take a seat however, the elevator chimed and in walked a man with beautiful light green eyes and a charming smile.

"You must be Mary Elizabeth. I'm sorry I'm late but I got stuck in traffic. I-10 seems to be getting worse every day. I'm David da Luca and I'll be working with you this week, getting you trained for your new position."

"It's so good to meet you Mr. da Luca and please call me Elizabeth."

"Alright Elizabeth, let's get you settled into your new office. It's right next to the boss's."

"I have to be honest, this is all a little overwhelming. I don't know how one man does it all."

"He's a brilliant man and I'm sure you'll enjoy working for him."

I laughed.

"I meant you Mr. da Luca. I don't know how you keep up with everything."

"It isn't easy, but you'll learn in time how to manage so many tasks at once."

"Do you work for Mr. Moretti as well," I asked.

"No, I work for one of the senior associates, Devlin Kent. You met Mrs. Sherman already at reception. She handles all of their phone calls and general emails for both Mr. Moretti and Mr. Kent. Like you will be doing, I handle everything for my boss to picking up his dry cleaning, to filing his paperwork, his emails, phone calls, his schedule and grabbing him lunch and sometimes dinner. You'll also book his meetings, arrange his travel and at times, buy gifts for his friends and family. You know, your typical assistant type duties."

"Sounds like a lot of work," I said teasingly -- still a little overwhelmed by how much they expected of me, but trying to play it off like I could so handle all of this.

"Get used to it. This is your life now. Starting today you'll be at Mr. Moretti's beckon call."

"Wait, what?"

"This isn't a nine to five job Miss Seabrook. I thought human resources explained all of this to you. If Mr. Moretti needs something at three am on Christmas Eve then you'll jump your pretty little head off of those fluffy pillows of yours and get it for him. If you can't handle that then you need to speak up now so we can find you a replacement."

"No, of course not. I look forward to the challenge. I assure you, I'll do whatever it takes."

"Good," he said as he opened the door to my new office. "That's exactly what I wanted to hear. I know this job won't be easy but it pays extremely well and the benefits are out of this world. You'll see."

I didn't quite know what he meant by that but for now I was just too overwhelmed with my new office to think to ask.

The office I would be sharing with Mr. da Luca, was small but breathtakingly beautiful. There were matching U shaped desks made of cherry wood with a matching hutch, file cabinet and a bookshelf that took up most of one of the walls filled with a variety of titles. It really was an ideal office.

The beige carpets were soft and several oversized plants were positioned throughout the room to give it a homey feeling. The office was a sharp contrast to the modern feel of the lobby. On the desk was my new laptop, iPad, and the latest iPhone.

"These are your lifeline. You keep them with you at all times. If Mr. Moretti needs you, he needs to be able to reach you. The iPhone and iPad both have solar chargers built into the cases so you shouldn't ever have 'my phone needed charging' as an excuse."

"Yes sir," I said as I gathered them up, placing the iPhone and iPad in my purse.

On the side of my desk was an overflowing in and out box.

"Let's get started," Mr. da Luca said as he took a seat and began going through the notes, organizing them by which needed attention first. Once the notes were ordered, I dug in and got started on the work.

By the early afternoon I began to pick up on some of the tasks and really enjoyed Mr. da Luca's company. We worked well together. After lunch we began the daunting task of cleaning out Mr. Moretti's email. I was glad to find I was able to do it on my own without much assistance needed from Mr. da Luca.

Just as I finished, we were interrupted.

"David, cancel my appointments for the rest of the day. I need to go handle something for my father. Before I leave, I also need those shipping channel reports if you've finished them."

I looked up as the most stunning man I'd ever seen walked through a connecting door on the east wall. He was distracted, looking at something on his iPad which gave me a few moments to check him out.

The first thing I noticed about him was his build. He was easily six foot four with broad shoulders, chiseled features and a sexy smile. As his arm moved, stretching the obviously expensive, well-tailored business suit, I could easily glean he was pure muscle, not an ounce of fat dare touch his perfect body. He looked like a God from one of those statues from ancient history.

He reached up and ran his fingers through his black hair, giving it a tussled look, making him even better looking.

Just then, he looked up and his silver eyes met my startled green ones.

"I'm sorry David, I forgot you had someone with you today."

I sat there frozen in place. I couldn't stop staring at the man.

"Devlin Kent," he said as he held his hand out to me.

"Holy smokes, I'm in trouble," was my only thought as I looked at his hand like it was a snake that was going to bite me. I knew I was supposed to take his hand and shake it but I just couldn't move.

As I hesitated an awkward amount of time, he raised his eyebrow at me questioningly. My face turned several shades of red as I finally broke eye contact. I snapped out of my trance, stood and gave him my hand.

"Hello, I'm Mary Elizabeth Seabrook."

As our hands touched, I felt a surge of electricity shoot through my body. I was rooted to the spot as his fingers closed around mine. The intensity between us was enough to leave me shaking, though I really hoped my fear wasn't showing through.

"Mary Elizabeth," he said softly, as if he was testing it out on his tongue. "I like it."

Normally at this point I would say something like 'please call me Elizabeth', but I couldn't seem to formulate a single word. All I could do was smile.

I knew the firm couldn't have been named for him because he not a partner. I remembered David saying earlier in the day, that his boss was a senior associate. But still, I couldn't help but wonder if he was somehow related to one of the founding partners because not only did he speak with a distinctly British accent, but his last name was Kent as in Ashworth and Kent. Maybe it was just a coincidence. Perhaps Kent was a common last name in England like Smith or Jones was here in America.

I didn't even know why it mattered. It didn't matter. It shouldn't matter. But it did. This man was all I could think about. The way he walked, the way he talked, the way he smelled, the way he smiled, the way his grey eyes sparkled when the light hit them just right. Oh my God, it's official. I've gone completely insane.

What I needed to be doing was focusing on my job. But with each passing day my secret obsession with Devlin Kent grew.

But the one thing I was not, was the kind of person who would act on their emotions. I knew better. I knew that this was the best job I'd had in my entire life and trying to date one of the senior associates could only be trouble and would probably cost me my job.

As much as I wanted the man, I wasn't going to risk my job over it.

Chapter 2

The next week I almost went into full blown panic mode when Mr. da Luca informed me he was going out of town and that I would have to pick up the slack in his absence with Mr. Kent, as well as my normal duties for Mr. Moretti. It was my second week and I was doing much better, but fear consumed me at the thought of Mr. da Luca leaving me on my own.

"Don't worry about it. You are going to be fine," he assured me.

But I knew that wasn't true. It was too soon. I needed more time before being left to my own devices. There was still so much I didn't know and now I would have to handle additional duties.

"If you need me, I'm only a phone call away. You can call me anytime you want, day or night."

That made me feel a little better, but still I was nervous. Mr. Moretti was such a demanding boss. One wrong move and he could fire me and I desperately needed this job. He wasn't exactly rude, but he hadn't been all that friendly either. I'd yet to see him smile.

Come to think of it, Mr. Kent was the same way. I hadn't seen him smile either, especially when he was looking at me.

"You are going to be fine, really. Just go down your daily checklist and mark things off as you complete each task. If he asks you for anything, add it to your list. It's really that simple."

I knew David was right, but it still didn't make me feel any better about being left alone with Mr. Moretti and Mr. Kent.

"Alright then, I'm off. Have a great week," Mr. da Luca said before heading out of the office.

I sat at my desk, feeling overwhelmed. But I had my assignments so I dove right in. A few hours later my intercom buzzed.

"Mary Elizabeth I need you in my office."

Mr. Kent was short and to the point. Clearly he wasn't going to win any congeniality awards any time soon.

I picked up my laptop, and quickly walked to his office.

"Good afternoon Mr. Kent."

"Put your things down over there," he said as he pointed to a small desk in the corner of his office.

I set my laptop on the tiny desk and took my seat.

"Do you know how to take dictation?"

"Of course."

I clicked the icon to open up Microsoft Word and positioned my fingers on the keys, waiting for him to begin.

"I need you to type up a few formal letters for me. I want you to type them up and then get them back to me within the hour. Remember to double, or even triple check them, to ensure there are no errors. Do you understand?"

"Of course Mr. Kent."

I had to stare at my computer, rather than look at him while I cursed my reaction to him. As his scent washed over me, my body, which seemed to have a mind of its own lately, tingled in anticipation of his touch.

I needed to get control of my emotions before I ended up doing something stupid like jumping on his lap or begging him to throw me over his desk. It wasn't like I was a hormone addled teenager so I couldn't understand why I was reacting so strongly to this man. I'd never done it before. Yes he was attractive but I'd been near countless hot guys before. Why this guy? And why now? I needed this job. I couldn't let something stupid like crushing on a co-worker or one of the bosses get in the way of my success at my first chance at a real job, a real career.

I'm almost twenty-one years old. I have my whole life ahead of me and lots of time to find love. Now was the time I needed to be focusing on my work. Love would come later. Love? Seriously? Oh God. This thing with Mr. Kent wasn't love. It was lust. I'm so ridiculous.

Finally I pulled myself together and took down everything he had to say. This wasn't the first time I had taken dictation, but it was most definitely the hardest. Trying to focus on what Mr. Kent was saying was damn near impossible.

"That will be all," he finally said.

"Okay, I'll have these done in a jiffy," I said nervously as I walked out the door and back to my own office.

Chapter 3

I stepped off the elevator with a big smile on my face. I'd been at my new job for over a month now and I was finally getting the hang of everything. I loved the work I was doing and felt confident that I was getting everything down pat. I was also getting to know some of the people from the office and it felt good to make friends. Mr. Moretti even smiled at me, not once but twice in the last few days.

As I turned the corner, heading towards my office I almost ran right smack into David da Luca.

"Hey now, be careful there."

"Oh my goodness, Mr. da Luca I'm so sorry. I wasn't paying attention to where I was going."

"I noticed," he replied teasingly.

"I'm so sorry."

"It's fine, really," he chuckled. "No harm, no foul." The corner of his lips turned up to a sexy smile.

I might not date a lot but I wasn't exactly unaware of the subtle signals he had been sending my way.

I looked at the man, really looked at him and wished I felt the tiniest spark of interest in him, but I didn't. And I didn't know why. He was normally the kind of guy I would date. He was well dressed, decent looking but not overwhelmingly so like Devlin Kent. David was a nice guy with a sense of humor.

He also didn't give me butterflies or make my cheeks flush. He was safe and he wasn't my boss. So why did the thought of going out with him make my stomach turn?

I glanced over my shoulder and noticed Devlin standing in his office door glaring daggers at me and David. I don't know why he would be upset, we were just chatting. It wasn't even anything someone might mistake as a casual flirt.

Sure I smiled at David as he talked to me, but I tried to smile at everyone. Everyone that is, that wasn't barking orders at me like Mr. Kent. Okay, maybe David da Luca was flirting with me a little, but what did Devlin care?

It irritated me that I cared what he thought. I tried to convince myself that he only did so because he knew office romances inevitably caused poor work performance when they went south. But truth of the matter was, I wanted him to care because he cared about me.

I wanted him to storm over to us and stake his claim on me. Which was completely ridiculous, I know. But hey, a girl can dream, right?

Later that day he called me into his office. When I came in and sat down, he stood up, looming over me. I sighed as I lifted my head to look at him, knowing he was in a mood.

"I don't like office romances. They cause nothing but trouble. Though it isn't a policy, it's greatly frowned upon." He informed me in his most stately tone of voice.

I had to silently count to ten before responding. I knew right away that he had seen Mr. da Luca flirting with me, but it wasn't my fault. I hadn't flirted back nor did I encourage his advances. It wasn't fair that Mr. Kent was coming down on me for something I didn't do.

"Thank you for letting me know about the company policy Mr. Kent but I don't think there is anyone here I would be interested in dating so I don't think this will be an issue with me."

Devlin opened his mouth to respond, then quickly shut it.

"Okay then Miss Seabrook. I just wanted to make sure you understood my feelings on the matter."

"Mr. Kent, I don't think who I date is really relevant to my job."

Suddenly he was inches from my face. "When you work for me Miss Seabrook you will listen to what I say."

"Well then Mr. Kent, it's a good thing I don't work for you then isn't it? If you recall, I work for Mr. Moretti."

That only seemed to infuriate him more.

"David da Luca is a womanizer and I don't want to deal with the repercussions when he throws you out with the trash the next day and believe me he will, that's just how he operates."

I leaned back trying to put a few inches between us, my heart beating uncontrollably. I suddenly found myself with the overwhelming urge to reach out and kiss him. I wanted Devlin Kent. Everything about him screamed sex and if he leaned in just another inch and claimed my mouth, I'd welcome it.

Okay, sure I knew it was irrational and I should have my head examined for lusting after him but I'd been dealing with the heat coming off of him in waves for a month now and I wondered if my imagination would do justice to what it might feel like to actually kiss him.

How bad could one kiss really be? At least then I'd figure out it was probably all in my imagination -- the sparks, the desire, the chemistry.

For what seemed like an eternity I couldn't break eye contact. I knew I couldn't follow through with my desire. Or could I? I could lean in that extra inch and taste his lips.

No, I can't. 'Look away,' I told myself.

Finally I found the willpower to turn my head, having no idea how long we had been there, face to face.

Realizing how close I'd come to closing that gap and kissing him, shocked me. I took a deep breath and willed my body to return to normal. I hadn't felt such an intense desire for a man before. I wasn't used to being this out of control.

If I hadn't found the willpower to break our eye contact I knew I would have kissed him and feared that single kiss would have sent me over the edge. I needed to regroup and expend some of this pent-up energy.

Chapter 4

On the first Friday of every month, most of the office would meet at the bar just down the street, for a drink. It was an Ashworth and Kent tradition, dating back to when the firm first opened in the early 1900s in England and apparently every location, still to this day, got together once a month.

While you weren't required to go, it was something the higher ups greatly encouraged. They felt it fostered a strong team spirit. In a way I really think it did. Everyone mingled with everyone else from the highest ranking partner to the lowliest mailroom clerk. They laughed and sang karaoke together and shared a beer like they were all old friends and not co-workers or employer and employees. It was nice.

While I was never really a big drinker, even I would have a glass of wine or two with everyone at the bar on the first Friday of every month, just like the rest of them.

At first I sat towards the end of one of the big tables, trying not to be noticed. But over time I started making friends and eventually really started to look forward to those Friday nights when we would all get together.

My best friend at the office was a girl named Sandy. While we didn't really work closely together, we always seemed to find each other come Friday night or any office social gathering.

She was quite a bit older than me and had been at Ashworth and Kent for more than ten years and she knew all the gossip. I think that's what I loved most about her. If you wanted to know who got in trouble or who was hooking up, all you had to do was find Sandy and get a few drinks in her. That girl couldn't keep a secret to save her life.

Which is why it was odd I would be stupid enough to confess my secret crush on Devlin Kent to her of all people.

"Alright girls, settle down," Sandy said. "It's time to get down to business."

All of the girls at the table giggled. We knew what that meant. It was time to play a round of rate your co-worker. And by co-workers of course that meant the sexy men in the office.

Sandy pulled out her notepad and started going down the list of names. We would all shout out a number, from one to ten to rank the person in question. Sometimes we would stop to explain why we rated the guy in question a certain way.

Edward Latimore, for example I ranked a six. Great ass, but horrible breath. The finest ass in the world couldn't make up for all that garlic the man ate.

Tina, another girl who typically sat at our table gave her boss, Mr. Bancroft a two, because he was always short with her, but the rest of us gave him a seven, because he was pretty sexy, so we could overlook his surly demeanor.

The one name all the girls agreed on was Devlin Kent. A perfect ten every time. He always won the game as the hottest man at Ashworth and Kent. Then again, how could he not with those steely grey eyes and rock hard body? He was the epitome of manliness and his British accent didn't hurt either.

Devlin was also the only man on our list that wasn't married or didn't date. At least not anyone from the office. As far as anyone knew, all the man ever did was work. If he did have a private life or dated anyone, nobody knew about it, not even Sandy.

And that's saying a lot because I don't think in the year I've now worked at Ashworth and Kent, I've ever heard of a single piece of gossip she didn't know about.

I think to some extent, every girl in the office had a thing for Devlin. It was hard not to. He was a very sexy man with broad shoulders and a dominating presence about him. When he was near, he owned the room. He spoke with authority and people around him paid attention. It's part of what made him such an amazing lawyer.

If the man said drop your panties, you would just do it. You wouldn't question him because he had that way about him that made you trust him and you knew that if he told you to do something, it was because it was the right thing to do.

Our game was interrupted by a drunken co-worker laughing loudly as another man looked down the front of her low cut dress. I wasn't a virgin, but I wasn't exactly the office slut either. That distinction fell to Brianna Bristow. She was the biggest whore and didn't seem to care that people knew that about her either. She was pretty enough I guess, and used her sexuality to try and get ahead or get what she wanted.

I can still remember the time I overheard her say, "Why bother working hard, when you can just show your tits?"

At first I was sure she had to be joking, but in time I learned that wasn't the case. Every time we went out on Friday nights, she would always go home with someone new. The one person she had never been able to land however, was Devlin. Then again, nobody else had either, including me.

That was not for a lack of trying on Brianna's part though. She flirted relentlessly with Devlin. And that alone was the reason why I hated her with a passion. Which was silly because it wasn't like Devlin was mine or that she or anyone else even knew I had a crush on him.

So it wasn't really fair that I held her flirting with him against her. Yet, logical or not, I still did. I couldn't help myself. When I saw her push her big fake breasts out to make sure than Devlin and every other man standing in front of her looked at them, my blood boiled.

This particular night, Brianna was in rare form. I wasn't sure if she was really drunk or just a great actress. As the night went on, she got louder and louder.

"Oh Devlin you are so funny. Oh Devlin you are just the best. Oh Devlin how do you not have a wife to take care of you yet?"

The more this went on, the more I drank and drank and drank.

"What's with you tonight?" Sandy asked.

"I don't know. I guess it's just been a rough week."

Sandy looked at me then followed my gaze to Devlin.

"Oh my God! How could you not tell me?"

"Tell you what?" I asked Sandy, confused by what she meant.

She leaned in so that nobody else could hear her. "That you are in love with Devlin Kent."

"What? No. Who told you that? That's ridiculous."

I quickly looked around, making sure that nobody overheard her.

"I can't believe you Elizabeth. Look at your face. It's bright red. You have the hots for ..."

I put my hand over her mouth so that she couldn't finish.

"Please Sandy. You can't tell anybody. I would just die if anyone knew."

"How long has this been going on?"

"I don't know, I guess awhile now," I admitted begrudgingly.

"How long Elizabeth," Sandy demanded to know.

I sighed. "Since the first day I met him."

Sandy was ecstatic, jumping up and down like a kid with a new toy. I however wanted to lay my head down on the table, clothes my eyes and pretend this never happened.

"How could I not have seen it? How could this escaped my radar all of this time?" Sandy wondered out loud.

I wanted to crawl under the table and die. But instead I just had another shot or two, or three.

I found that the more I drank, the easier it was not to turn my head and watch what was going on at Devlin's table. Instead I focused on the other men in the bar, who kept buying the girls at our table drinks.

Just as another round of shots were delivered to our table I felt a strong hand on my shoulder. Then warm breath in my ear.

"I think you've had enough tonight Mary Elizabeth."

I looked up to see Devlin standing over me. But before I could respond, he grabbed my wrist, pulled me up from my chair.

"Get your things. It's time to go," he commanded and I obeyed.

I snagged my purse and did my best to keep up as he dragged me out the door of the bar.

"Where are we going?" I asked when we got outside.

"I'm taking you home. You've had far too much to drink tonight."

"I'm fine Devlin. You don't have to babysit me. You can go back in and do whatever it was you were doing with Brianna."

He pushed my back against the passenger side door of his car. Then he leaned over me, with a hand on either side of me, effectively caging me in.

"Do you really think I want to spend another minute with Brianna Bristow?"

He towered over me and all I could do was look up at him, into his mesmerizing grey eyes. For just a moment I was sure he was going to lean down and kiss me. Instead he unlocked his door, put me in the seat, and even fastened my seatbelt before he climbed in the driver's side and started the car.

I wanted to ask where we were going but I was too stunned to speak. I was in the car with Devlin Kent and he almost kissed me. Maybe. Possibly. Probably.

I glanced down and noticed on the little clock in his dashboard that it was after ten. I don't normally stay at the bar for more than an hour. How in the world did so much time get away from me?

We drove through the city streets and Devlin didn't say a word. It was dark outside and his tented windows made it even harder to see, so I couldn't really tell where it was we were headed. Did he know where I live or was he taking me to his place?

I couldn't stand the silence anymore and finally I spoke up. "Where are you taking me?"

He didn't answer, at least not at first.

"I'm taking you to my place so you can sleep this off."

"I'm fine Devlin, really. You don't have to take care of me."

"Apparently I do. I watched exactly how much you had to drink tonight. What were you thinking? Any one of those men could have taken advantage of you."

He was angry with me.

"Devlin I'm an adult. Old enough to drink and vote and even buy cigarettes if I was so inclined. I don't need a babysitter."

He didn't respond. He just kept driving. But when I glanced over at him, I could see a muscle in his jaw tick.

It was like he was trying his best to maintain his calm with me. Was I really that out of control at the bar? I didn't think so and I was nowhere near the level Brianna had been.

Okay it's true I was drunk, more so than I had ever been in my life. But it wasn't like I was dancing naked on the tables or anything. I was just sitting there laughing with my friends from work, letting a few guys flirt with us and buy us drinks. Was that really so bad?

Before I could debate the issue with him further, we pulled into a parking garage and into one of the available spaces. He got out of the car and went to open my door. I wasn't moving though. I wanted to know what was going on.

"Devlin, this is ridiculous. Just take me home."

He apparently wasn't in the mood to argue with me because he unfastened my seatbelt, picked me up, threw me over his shoulder and walked me to the elevator. Once inside I insisted he let me down but he wasn't having any of it.

We rode all the way to the top floor with me like that and when we got inside of his place, he finally flopped me down unceremoniously on his couch.

"You are such a caveman," I yelled at him.

"What is wrong with you Devlin? You can't just throw a girl over your shoulder like that and take her up to your apartment."

He chuckled. "Apparently I can."

Did he seriously just laugh at me?

"You are such a pig Devlin! Take me home."

"You aren't going anywhere Mary Elizabeth. It's late, I'm tired and you've had far too much to drink to be on your own tonight."

And that was that. Apparently I was going to stay the night at Devlin's place.

"Now let's get you settled," he said as if the matter had been settled.

When I didn't move, he came over to me, picked me up and carried me to the bedroom. He sat me down on the bed gently and then handed me a t-shirt from his closet. It was far too big for me, but still comfortable and smelt just like him.

"I can't sleep," I said softly. "Will you stay with me for a little while?"

He sighed but did join me on the bed, with his clothes still on. He positioned me in the crook of his arm.

"Why aren't you married," I asked.

"Ssssh," he responded. "Close your eyes and get some rest."

I wanted to know more about him but the more I laid there, the heavier my eyes got, until finally sleep overtook me.

I don't know how long he stayed with me but when I awoke, he was gone and I was alone in his bed. Was this his bed? Or was this a guest room? It seemed more like a guest room than a master bedroom.

Chapter 5

When I sat up I realized just how horrible I felt. My head was killing me, my eyes felt like someone was poking me with needles and my throat was dry. I immediately flopped back down on the pillow, deciding that I wasn't ready to get up, just yet.

Before long I heard a noise in the other room. It had to be Devlin. What was he doing? There were some faint banging noises and some other strange sounds I couldn't quite make out.

Curiosity finally got the best of me so I got out of bed and followed the noises into what turned out to be the kitchen.

"Good morning sunshine. How you feeling," Devlin asked cheerfully.

I just grunted. Truth was I felt like shit. He was right, I drank way to much the night before but I wasn't about to admit that to him now.

"Sit down. Breakfast is almost ready."

I did as I was told, without giving it a second thought. When I sat down however, I couldn't help but laugh. It was just amazing how this man could give a simple command and people followed him blindly. He had such an authoritative way about him.

"What's so funny," he asked.

"Nothing. Everything. I don't know."

"Well which is it," he asked as he sat a plate of eggs and bacon in front of me.

"This looks delicious. I didn't know you could cook."

"I'm sure there is quite a bit about me that you don't know," Devlin responded playfully.

"I don't know. I probably know more about you than you think."

Devlin eyed me skeptically.

"You'd be surprised how much the ladies in the office talk about you."

"I think you ladies have far too much free time on your hands." Devlin chuckled and then went back to eating his breakfast.

After eating breakfast, downing a big glass of orange juice and two glasses of water, I started to feel almost human again.

"I'm sorry about last night Devlin. I feel bad that you had to spend your Friday night babysitting me."

"Let's get you dressed so we can go pick up your car."

I followed him into the bedroom and gathered my clothes.

"I don't have a car Devlin."

"What do you mean you don't have a car? How do you get to work then?"

"I take the bus."

"Why don't you have a car? I know I've seen you in the parking garage before."

"My car broke down a few weeks ago and I just haven't been able to get it repaired yet."

"You were going to take the bus home last night, at that hour," Devlin asked.

"No, if I stay late I take a cab home. If I don't catch the six pm bus then I will miss my transfer."

"Transfer? So you take more than one bus to get to work, and you've been doing this for weeks?"

"Yes. I don't have the money to fix my car yet."

"What's wrong with it?"

"It's an old car. There are a lot of things wrong with it. The transmission is just the latest in a long line of problems."

"Come on, get your clothes on," Devlin said as he walked out the door, leaving me to get dressed on my own.

Dressed, I walked out and Devlin led me through his apartment, to the elevator and down to his car. I gave him my address, he programmed it into his GPS and we were off.

When we pulled into the parking lot of my apartment complex he found a parking spot and turned off his car.

"This is where you live?"

"Yes. I don't make what you do Devlin. The rent is cheap. It's all I can afford."

"I'm sorry Mary Elizabeth. I didn't mean to upset you. I just don't like the thought of you in a place like this."

"Let's go," Devlin said as he helped me out of the car.

"Where are we going?"

"To pack your clothes."

"Why are we packing my clothes?"

Although he didn't answer my question, I led him into my tiny little apartment anyway, which thank goodness was clean. I began to do as he told me to do and packed a suitcase and then grabbed my makeup case.

"Is that all you are bringing with you?" Devlin asked while looking down at my two bags.

"I only have the one suitcase. Why do I need so many clothes anyway? Where are we going?"

"Come on, let's go," Devlin said as he drug me out the front door of my apartment and back to his car, still not answering my question about where in the world we were going.

I went with him to the car, let him help me to my seat and even fasten my seatbelt for me like I was some sort of child. But I had enough so before he started the car, I demanded to know where he was taking me and why.

"I'm not letting you stay at this place anymore," he said with a disgusted look on his face as he gestured towards my apartment building.

I knew I didn't live in the best place, but it wasn't that bad. It was clean and for the most part my neighbors were quiet. What more could I ask for, with the kind of rent I was paying? It bugged me that he was judging me like that. I was doing the best I could do with the little money I had. Sure I had a good job, but that was a good job for me. I wasn't making near the money he was. I probably made a year what he made in a month.

"And where do you suppose I live Devlin? I can't afford a fancy penthouse like you."

Devlin sighed, started the car and we drove away. I guess that was the end of that conversation. And yet I still had no idea where he was taking me.

After a silent twenty minute drive, we pulled into the parking garage at his building.

"Why didn't you tell me we were going back to your place?" I asked.

"Why must you ask so many questions? Can't you just trust that I have your best interests at heart?"

I really didn't know what to say to that. What could I say to that? 'Sorry Devlin, but I ask too many questions because I'm too fucked up in the head to trust that anyone really cares about me.' Yeah that would go over well.

We walked into his building in silence. This time, I actually paid attention. It really was a lovely place. The lobby was a bright, open space with lots of light. We got into the oversized elevator and he entered a keycard to allow him access to the top floor. I didn't even notice he did that the first time.

I knew lawyers made good money, but I doubt most could afford this kind of spread. No, he had to have family money. His penthouse was just too much to be able to afford it on his salary alone. He wasn't even a partner.

The elevator opened up directly into his foyer which led to a large ornate door. As we walked through the door Devlin told me to sit as he pointed to the overstuffed couch in the living room. So I sat and waited as he took my bags somewhere. I assumed the bedroom. When he returned he had a velvet covered box with him.

"Remove your clothes," he commanded.

"Excuse me?"

"You haven't earned the right to wear them."

Has he lost his ever loving mind? Surely he's just joking.

"Devlin I'm not going to get naked for you."

"Yes, you are."

"I don't know what kind of game you are playing Devlin, but it's not funny."

"It's not meant to be."

"I've had my eye on you for a long time Mary Elizabeth and I've decided I want you for my slave."

I wanted to say something but he just pressed a finger against my lips.

"From here on out you will address me as Master. The only words I expect to hear from you are yes Master or no Master."

At first I thought he was just teasing me but when he didn't laugh I realized he was completely serious about this.

"I am going to take this weekend to train you. If you do not obey me you will be punished."

A host of images suddenly flashed through my mind. I'd never been spanked before, even as a child, when your mother works all the time, she doesn't really have time for things like discipline.

This can't be right. He couldn't really be serious, could he? I looked at him, completely astonished.

"What the hell are you talking about Devlin? Have you lost your mind?"

Before I knew what was happening he pulled me across his lap, pushed my dress up, ripped off my panties and began spanking me, like I was a little girl and he had to punish me for being naughty.

"I told you to address me as Master. You will learn to do as you are told."

"Please stop. Why are you doing this?" I cried.

He didn't listen to me though. He just continued to spank me until my ass was on fire.

I was so confused but at the same time, so aroused and a tiny bit excited. I knew I should be mad at what he was doing to me, but deep down, somewhere in the darkest part of my subconscious, I liked it.

Am I a freak? Is something totally wrong with me that I loved what he was doing to me?

His hand moved from my very red behind to my pussy and to my horror I was wet. I don't know how to explain it, this kind of thing wasn't sexy to me yet my body apparently thought differently. He played with my clit rubbing his thumb against it and I felt myself squirming under his touch. But before things could get too heated he let me go and I slid over to the other end of the sofa, trying to put as much distance between us as I could.

"Now do you understand that you are here to do as I say?"

My mind was in a whirl. I couldn't understand how all of this was happening and what made him think it was okay to treat me like that. I'm not that kind of girl. I don't like spankings or bondage or any of those kinky things. Yet despite that, I still begrudgingly answered him with a "Yes Master". I don't know what came over me and why I did it. I felt foolish as soon as I said the words.

"Now, the first rule as my slave is you are to be naked at all times, so take off your clothes."

I did as he told me. I stood up and removed my dress and then my bra. He had already ripped my panties off so now all I had on was my high heels.

"Come stand in front of me," he ordered and I reluctantly obeyed.

He held a riding crop in his hand now. I stood where he had indicated and looked pleadingly at him, wondering what he was going to do next. He reached out and struck me across the thighs with it. The pain convinced me that he was deadly serious about this whole master and slave thing. I could barely believe all of this was really happening. I've known Devlin for about a year now and I'd never seen this side of him. He was always so different at work -- always in control and together.

He continued to hit me with the crop and all I could do was cry. I was unsure of what to do or say. I just wanted this whole ordeal to be over. Why was he doing this to me?

"You won't be needing these," he said as he picked up the clothes from the floor and placed them in a neat pile on the sofa.

I stood there, too scared to move a muscle as he opened the velvet covered box he brought in the room with him earlier. Inside was a leather collar which he fastened around my neck.

"That's better," he said. "Now you are beginning to look like a slave. However, we still have to teach you to behave properly."

He attached a leash to the collar, as if I was some animal he was going to take on a walk in the park.

"Get on the floor and crawl on your hands and knees."

When I hesitated I felt the sting of the crop on my thighs and dropped down on all fours. When he tried to lead me round the room, I balked and refused to crawl.

"I see we are going to have to do this the hard way."

He hit me again with the riding crop and I began to tear up again. I didn't want to cry, I wanted to be strong and not let him know he was getting to me, but the pain was just too much.

"What did I tell you about disobeying me?"

I remained silent and once more the crop slashed across my ass.

"You said I would be punished," I murmured. The crop came down with a stinging force across my thighs before I realized my mistake.

"What did you say?" he demanded. "I'm sure you can do better than that."

"You said I would be punished Master."

"That's better, don't make the same mistake again."

"No Master, I won't." I obediently replied.

"You will have to be punished for your earlier refusal."

"Please no," I begged. "This is all just too much. I can't take any more."

He didn't listen to my pleas. It was as if I hadn't spoken. Instead he picked me up and carried me over to the long table in his dining room. It was the one we had just eaten breakfast on that very morning. What I didn't notice then was that there were metal rings set part way down the polished surface, one on either side. Now it was all I could seem to see about the table.

He bent me over the table and fastened my wrists to the rings. I was now bent over with my ass exposed and completely helpless. I struggled against my restraints but it was no use, I couldn't get free.

Devlin came up behind me and ran his hand over my behind. I tried to turn around to see what he was doing, but I was secured with the rings to the table. All I could do was wait and see what he was going to do to me. I didn't have to wait long to find out what Devlin had in mind. Soon he came up until he was level with my face and showed me what he had in his hand. He was holding a leather paddle.

I cried out as he landed the first of what would be many strokes. The paddle had a vicious sting and I was soon crying out for mercy.

"Does that feel good?"

I didn't answer him, so he smacked my ass again with the paddle.

"I said, does that feel good?"

"Yes, Master," I responded through gritted teeth. Unable to hold back the tears that now flowed freely down my face.

"When I ask you a question you will answer without hesitation or you will be punished further."

"Yes, Master."

He ran his hand over my reddened behind and then down my thigh. He pushed my legs outwards, spreading them out wider, so he could gain total access to those concealed areas of my buttocks.

"You do have a sweet little ass. You are going to make a great slave."

"Please just let me go. I won't tell anyone what you've done. We'll just pretend all of this never happened. Please. It doesn't have to be like this."

"I didn't say you could speak."

I angered him by begging him to free me and he began spanking my ass with the paddle again over and over. The sting was unbearable. All I could do is cry and pray it would be over soon.

"You will learn not to speak unless spoken to."

"Yes, Master," I murmured. "I'm sorry Master."

"I can't hear you," he said just before smacking the paddle on my bare ass one more time.

"Yes, Master," I said, much louder this time.

"I don't want to hurt you my sweet little slave, it's just the only way to ensure your obedience."

I started to beg for my freedom again, but the pain in my ass reminded me that wasn't a good idea. Instead I just responded with what I knew he wanted to hear.

"Yes, Master."

"That's a good girl," he praised before continuing to rub his hand across my ass, examining his handy work.

"Do you understand why you were being punished?"

"Yes Master. Because I was naughty."

"That's a good girl," he soothed.

He moved his hand lower and slipped two fingers inside of me. As much as I hated to admit it, he was quite skilled and it felt good, really good and before I knew it, my traitorous body had begun to react to his touch. I was wet for him and I didn't want him to stop.

He leaned over my body, so that he could whisper in my ear, while he continued to stimulate my clit. "Do you like that?"

"Yes, Master."

"Do you want me to continue?"

"Yes, Master."

I let out a soft moan and he began rubbing my pussy harder and faster.

"You're a naughty girl, aren't you?"

"Yes, Master, oh God, yes."

I could feel my orgasm building. I couldn't believe it, here I was bound to a table, brutally beaten and now I'm about to get off. Still, I couldn't help it, my body wanted him, and there was nothing I could do to stop it. My breathing became erratic and I arched my back, desperately wanting more before finally it was all just too much.

"Enjoy yourself?" He asked with a bit of a sarcastic tone.

I was too breathless to reply, but yes I did enjoy myself and the waves of pleasure that were still washing over me.

"The problem is, I didn't say you could come. You are my slave and you will come only when given permission to do so."

Before I could ask if he was serious, Devlin leaned down and showed me his new weapon. Gone was the paddle and in its place was a cane, an actual bamboo cane.

Surely he wouldn't really hit me with it. This had to be just something he was going to use to scare me into submission. But I was wrong.

I heard a swish and then I felt the cane land across my backside, and the pain shot through me like a line of fire. I screamed out but it didn't do any good. He waited a few moments for the pain to sink in before laying another stroke across the back of my thighs.

There were tears running down my face and I sobbed as yet another stroke cut across my ass. I lost count of the strokes after that and could do nothing but endure each one as it slashed across my helpless bottom.

"Just remember, every time you disobey me, this is what is waiting for you."

"Please, I'm sorry Master. I won't do it again."

He paid no attention to my pleas and continued to beat me with the cane. I nearly passed out from the pain and barely noticed when he stopped and freed my wrists. He lifted me up and carried me semi-conscious into one of the bedrooms and handcuffed me to the bed so that I couldn't get away.

I was weak and tired and in a state of utter disbelief. My body hurt and I just wanted to close my eyes and go to sleep and make all of this go away. My eyes were heavy and I couldn't force myself to stay awake any longer even if I tried.

I don't know how long I was out but when I woke up, I was confused about where I was and what had happened. My body hurt all over, but especially my ass. It was only when I heard his footsteps retreating down the hall that I began to remember flashes of what had gone on. He must have come to check up on me and thought I was still asleep. Bit by bit, it came back to me what had happened. How I had been brought here, stripped, collared and beaten. I remembered how I was at the mercy of this man, who I thought I knew and trusted but he turned out to be a monster.

I heard his footsteps again and closed my eyes feigning sleep, hoping he thought I was still asleep and go away. No such luck.

I felt the coolness of a wet cloth on my forehead and opened my eyes to see him looking down at me. He had a look of concern on his face, which I found difficult to understand considering the thrashing he had given me. He, however, acted as if the punishment hadn't happened and gently wiped my face.

"In time you'll learn my sweet, that once a punishment had been administered, you're absolved of your misbehavior and it won't be mentioned again."

He smiled at me then undid the cuffs. He scooped me up in his arms and laid with me on the bed. It was then I noticed all the fluffy pillows and how nice the sheets where. My bruised body appreciated their softness.

He leaned in and kissed me. I knew there was no point in resisting him so I returned his kiss with equal fervor. I would do anything to avoid the risk of another beating. If he wanted a kiss then I would kiss him. If he told me to jump up and down on one leg while singing then that is what I would do. Nothing was worth risking another beating with the cane.

"My sweet little slave, you're going to find the balance between pleasure and pain."

I didn't want to find out more about that, I just wanted to go home. I wanted all of this to be over. Devlin may be the most gorgeous man I'd ever seen in my life, but looks aren't everything.

That's a lesson I have learned the hard way. I can't believe I had to have it beaten into me, but now I truly know not to judge a book by its cover.

Devlin is a monster, about as far from Prince Charming as one could get. Why did I ever think he was so perfect just because he was good looking?

Still, I had never felt so drawn to a man before. I had a hard time controlling my desire for him when he was around. Even when he was being a jerk of a boss at work, I was still attracted to him in a way I couldn't explain.

And now I'm naked, handcuffed to his bed, beaten and bruised and wondering if he is ever going to let me go.

Devlin ran his hand lightly over my breasts. He lowered his head and sucked on each nipple for a short time.

"Why are you doing this to me?" I asked, while trying to hold back my tears.

"Because I can. You are my slave, my property and that means I can do whatever I want to you."

I wanted to resist but I knew better, the pain wasn't worth it. For now he was my Master and I his slave.

Chapter 6

I must have slept the rest of the night because when I opened my eyes sunlight was pouring in through a window. I tried to stretch my arms but I realized I was still handcuffed to the bed. Only one wrist was restrained and I could move in a limited fashion. I rubbed my eyes with my free hand. I was alone in the big bed and struggled to sit up.

I was able to pull myself up with my free hand and managed to get a pillow between my back and the iron bars of the bed frame. I saw the welts on my thighs and grimaced at the memory of what happened the night before.

I could hear Devlin in another room. Surely he could not intend to keep me here as his slave forever. He's a lawyer, he had to know the legal ramifications of keeping me a prisoner. At some point he was going to have to let me return to my apartment, plus I had to go to work tomorrow so I took solace in knowing this nightmare would be over soon. Too many people from work seen us leave the bar together Friday night so if I went missing, they would go right to him. He had to know that, right?

It's going to be weird seeing him at the office after what he did to me last night. Maybe I should consider getting another job. I hate to leave Ashworth and Kent but I think it's just going to be too strange to see Devlin day in and day out after all of this. And there was no way I could face Sandy. I'm a horrible liar and I know the first time she sees me she'll ask me a million questions about what happened between Devlin and I after we left the bar. What could I say?

No, I just couldn't do it. I would have to get a new job. Somehow.

The smell of fresh coffee brewing in the other room brought me back to reality. I wanted a cup, but was afraid to call out to him and ask. Before long I heard his footsteps coming towards the bedroom and shortly after he appeared at the door, carrying a large tray. He balanced the tray on the bed and smiled down at me.

"Good morning my sweet little slave."

"Good morning Master"

"I thought you might like some breakfast."

He sat down on the bed and I thought he would release me so I could eat. However he made no move to free me. He poured two cups of coffee and asked me if I took cream and sugar.

"Cream but not sugar, Master."

He added the cream, stirred the coffee and held the cup up to my mouth so I could drink and I did so gratefully. There was a plate of croissants on the tray. He picked one up, tore a piece off and spread it with butter and jam, then fed it to me. Piece by piece he fed me the croissant stopping only to wipe my mouth with a napkin. The food was good and my empty stomach was grateful but it still felt strange being fed like a helpless child. While we ate he also handed me a small container with some pills. One I recognized as my birth control pill but I was unsure of what the others were and I looked at them closely, fearing what they could be.

"That's just a daily vitamin and the larger clear one is fish oil. It's supposed to enhance your immune system and help reduce inflammation."

It was strange to think that my kidnapper was concerned with my health and wellbeing but nonetheless I swallowed the pills and thanked him.

"Do you need to go to the restroom?"

"Yes please, Master, I do."

He smiled, clearly happy with my obedience. Pulling the key out of his pocket he unlocked the handcuff tethering me to the bed.

"You may take your time in there, have a shower, and wash your hair. However, there is no lock on the door and as my slave, you have no right to privacy. I can and will come in as I please."

"Yes, Master." I replied desperate now to relieve my bladder.

"The bathroom is through that door over there."

He motioned to a door on the other side of the room. I was not happy about the lack of privacy but there was not much I could do about it. All I could do is pray he wouldn't come in while I was on the toilet.

When I had finished using the potty, I stood up and looked around the bathroom. There were large full length mirrors hanging on the walls giving me a view of my bruised and beaten body from all angles. I examined the painful welts and seen for the first time just how bad of a thrashing I had taken last night.

Before I could obsess too much about it, I saw the door being pushed open and grabbed a towel to cover myself.

"What's this? Not being shy are we my slave?"

Devlin removed the towel from my grasp and pushed me down on my knees.

My face turned red as I realize he was standing over me naked. I don't know why seeing his body embarrassed me, but it did. I tried to turn away but as I felt his large cock brushing up against my face I got turned on. He really was a gorgeous man and having him stand there so close to me made my entire body tingle.

I opened my mouth to take him in and he tangled his hands in my hair. Pushed my head down, forcing me to take more of him in my mouth. As I sucked on his cock he began to make soft little noises that turned me on immensely. I started to tease his cock with my tongue, running it up and down his shaft and then stopping for just a moment to lick his balls. That made him groan louder and when he did, he took a tight grasp of my hair. I concentrated on the head of his cock and licked around the rim and when I did I felt him grow even larger in my mouth.

His hips were thrusting back and forth and he began pushing my head down on his cock even more. His soft little sexy noises returned and I knew he had to be close to coming. It was all so arousing I found myself reaching between my legs and rubbing my clit.

Without warning he withdrew from my mouth and in one quick motion, had me lying on my stomach on the bathroom floor. He was positioned directly behind me, his knees keeping my legs spread apart. His hands made contact with my bare ass and the sound of the hit reverberated around the whole room. My body tensed and tears stung my eyes.

"I didn't give you permission to play with yourself, did I?"

"No, Master. I'm sorry Master, I was just …"

Before I could finish trying to explain he spanked me yet again.

Tears flowed freely down my face. Devlin began to caress my ass, soothing the sting.

"You have such a nice little ass."

"Thank y…. "

My words were cut off and replaced with a loud scream as Devlin's hand made contact with my bare skin yet again.

"Don't tense up, it will only make it hurt more. You need to learn to relax and accept your punishment."

His voice was low and soothing, as if he had never hurt me. How could he be so gentle and sweet one moment and so brutal the next?

"Yes, Master," was all I could say.

He trailed his finger down the crack of my ass and then made his way to my pussy. He worked his finger up the length of my wet folds. He spread my lips and began gently rubbing my clit and I couldn't help but moan and push against him, wanting more. He pulled his hand out and spanked me.

"You are a greedy little girl aren't you? You are going to learn to appreciate what I give you."

He spanked me again, and I knew by now my ass had to be several shades of red. Although it was only his bare hand spanking me, instead of the paddle or cane from the previous night, it still hurt. I could feel the heat emanating from my skin.

"Yes, Master."

I felt his erection pushing up against my thigh. As much as he was hurting me for some reason my body still wanted him inside of me. I instinctively arched my back, wanting him to penetrate me.

"You are such a dirty little slut. Look at you, begging me to fuck you."

I didn't respond. What could I say? He was right, I did want him to fuck me.

He spanked my ass even harder. "Say it," he commanded. "Tell me what you want me to do to you."

I let out a yelp when his hand came down on my bare ass yet again.

"Say it!"

"I want you to fuck me Master," I murmured.

He spanked me again. "Say it like you mean it."

This time I spoke much louder. "I want you to fuck me hard and make me like it Master."

"You dirty little whore. You aren't worthy of my cock inside you."

"Please Master. I promise I'll be a good girl. I just want you to make me come."

His hands parted the cheeks of my ass and then I felt the sensation of his tongue on my asshole, probing and licking. The feeling was overwhelmingly arousing. I was quickly spinning out of control. The feeling of his large cock pushing against my leg, his tongue licking my asshole, it was all just so exquisite.

He brought one hand round and found my swollen clit. He toyed with it gently, pushing two fingers into my pussy and finger fucked me until I nearly came. It all drove me wild. I felt so full with lust for this man. I could barely stand it.

I let out a half moan and half whimper. What he was doing to me was so erotic and confusing and unbelievable. I didn't normally get off on the twisted stuff, it's just not me. This was more than I felt my body could take. I was so close to coming but then I remembered what Devlin had said last night about not coming without permission.

"Please slow down, I'm going to come," I begged.

"You better not," he said as he withdrew his hand.

I thrust my hips back, trying to get him to put his fingers back inside of me. I was close, so close, and I needed him inside of me badly.

He began spanking my ass with his bare hand over and over again. It hurt, I was aware of the pain but at the same time I was so aroused it was a different kind of feeling this time. The pain was somehow mixed in with the pleasure and the desire to come.

He reached between my legs again and rolled my clit between his thumb and forefinger. I couldn't hold back any more and cried out in pleasure. My pussy clutched in abandoned bliss and shock after shock of ecstasy went through me.

After Devlin stood up and helped me up from the floor and carried me to the bed, this time without securing my wrist to the bedframe with the handcuffs.

"You came didn't you?"

"Yes, Master," I said as I hung my head in shame.

"And what did I tell you about coming without permission?"

"You said I would be punished, Master."

"Yes, and so you shall be. This infraction will be going into your punishment book. I take note of each time you disobey me and at the end of the day, you will be punished for your transgressions. Do you understand?"

His eyes grew cold. "There will be no exceptions or excuses. Every time you disobey, baulk at something or talk out of turn it will be noted in the book."

"Yes, Master."

I understood but didn't agree with it. This wasn't right. He can't keep me prisoner like this. I'm not his slave. I'm a human being. But still, remembering last night's punishment with the cane, for now I better be careful not to anger him. I don't want to ever go through that again.

His face lost its stern look. "I think it's time we took a shower, you feel strong enough for that?"

"Yes, Master. Thank you."

He helped me out of bed and led me to the shower. First he washed himself then turned his attention to me, soaping me up from head to toe. He had an amazingly gentle touch as he washed my body and then my hair.

When we finished our shower, he enveloped me in a warm dry towel. With one fluid motion, he scooped me up and carried me back to the bed. He handcuffed my wrist to the bed frame while he finished drying my body with the towel then left the room with me shackled to the bed.

I heard him moving about the apartment and could do nothing but wait and see what was going to happen next. After a bit, he reappeared, freshly shaved and dressed.

"I have to go out for a while."

Surely he did not intend to go out and leave me chained to the bed for heaven knows how long. He undid the handcuffs and I thought for a moment he was going to relent. However, he slipped the cuffs through a bar on the bed and fastened them around both wrists so I found myself lying on my back, hands cuffed above my head.

"No please, you can't be serious."

He had a devious grin on his face. He was serious. I was helpless, cuffed to the bed and unable to do anything except endure the agony while he left and did God only knows what and for God only knows how long.

"What you don't seem to understand is that you are mine. Your body is mine, all of it, your mouth, your sweet little perky tits, your tight little pussy, your ass, all mine. I'm going to take you when I want, where I want and how I want. I'm going to do whatever I want with you because you now belong to me. You are my slave, my property."

He leaned down and kissed me on the forehead. "I won't be too long my slave. Try to be a good girl in my absence."

All I could do was cry as he left me alone. I heard the front door shut and the sound of the lock click and began to sob uncontrollably. I don't know how long I lay there like that. It felt like forever.

I was only aware of the pain and every minute felt like an hour. I tried twisting my body to find a position that might lessen the pain, but had no luck. No matter how I contorted by body, my arms hurt. All I could do is lie there, in agony, praying for his return. The longer it took, the heavier my arms got.

After what seemed like an eternity, I heard his key in the lock. He did not come straight into the bedroom though. I had no idea what he was doing but waited, tears pouring down my face. Finally, he came to check on me.

"Please Master," I begged him.

"What?" He teased, knowing full well what anguish I was in. "You want me to let your arms down?"

"Yes Master, please."

"Very well then, I suppose I can do that. I think by now you have learned your lesson."

"I will do anything you ask of me, please just let me put my arms down. The pain is unbearable."

He tugged at my wrists and then undid the handcuffs, letting my hands fall to my lap. After, he pulled something out of his pocket. I noticed it was the same leash from the night before.

"I hope we are not going to have any more trouble with this today," he said as he attached it to my collar.

"No, Master."

As soon as I got off the bed and onto my feet he pushed me down onto my knees.

"Now, I want you to crawl."

I did not hesitate this time but it still wasn't quick enough for him. The riding crop was back in his hand and the sting of it across my thighs started me moving. I crawled across the floor, following his lead with the slash of the crop urging me on. He led me into the living room and while I crawled on my hands and knees to where he wanted me to go I began to think about ways I could escape. I tried to play back the memory of walking into the building.

I tried to remember everything I could about it. There were mailboxes on the wall on the first floor and I didn't recall seeing a security guard in the lobby, nor did we use any sort of key to enter the front door.

That was good because if I did get away that meant I would easily be able to get out of the building. I remember walking into the elevator, that he called a lift.

I didn't think much of it at the time, but I've noticed over the years he did that sometimes, say some things differently like tennis shoes he called trainers. I always thought it was cute when he did that.

But just because I noticed a few things about him, didn't mean I really knew the man. We worked together every day for over a year. I knew how he liked his coffee, and that most days he wouldn't go out to eat lunch unless he was with a client. He tended to bring his lunch from home and it always seemed to be something healthy. I knew that on Monday he wore a red power tie. I knew when his birthday was and that his favorite cake was double chocolate. But now I realize all of those little things I knew about him were trivial and meaningless because I didn't really know him at all.

I had no idea where he was born, if he had siblings or where his parents lived. I knew he was a lawyer, so obviously he went to law school, but I didn't know where. Funny how easy it is to convince yourself that you know the people you see day in and day out at work, but really don't know them at all.

I tried to keep my focus on the layout of his building. He lives on the top floor, so I couldn't jump out a window. I might break my neck and kill myself. There had to be a better way to escape. Then it hit me, did he have one of those outdoor fire escapes like you see in movies? If he did and if I could find it, maybe that is how I could get away.

Even if I couldn't get enough time to run down all those flights of stairs, I could get down far enough to jump to safety. Maybe. How many flights could one jump and survive?

Then I looked down at my naked body and sighed. No clothes. If I did get lucky enough to get free I might have to do it naked. Thinking about facing an escape buck ass naked, I began to cry again. He turned and smacked the crop down hard on my ass.

"Stop crying or I'll give you something to really cry about."

"Yes, Master."

"Stand up."

I quickly obeyed and as I got to my feet he pushed my face against the wall and ordered me to stay. Several hooks were screwed into the wall. The sight of the clamps made my heart race.

He took out a long thin rope and began threading it through the hooks and around my wrists, with my arms stretched above my head and then he kicked my ankles forcing me to spread my legs wide while he connected my ankles to the hooks.

He unclipped the leash and left me standing there, completely exposed and unprotected. He could do as he wished with me and there was nothing I could do to defend myself.

I was scared, more so than I had been before. I wanted to cry but I remembered his warning and feared the beating I would get if I did. I took slow deep breaths, trying to control my fear and to stop myself from having an all-out panic attack.

Devlin picked up a strange looking whip with several leather strands, almost like the head of a mop, well if a mop was made out of leather.

"Do you know what this is?"

"No Master, I don't."

"This is a flogger."

As soon as he said it, he hit me across the breasts with it. It stung but didn't hurt as bad as the cane. He struck me again on each arm and then on the lower part of my stomach.

I could feel the tears starting to form in my eyes, each time he hit me with the flogger. I tried so hard to maintain control but the sting of the leather hitting my bare skin was just too much. I began to cry out in earnest and pulled at the restraints trying to get free as he continue to hit me with the flogger over and over again.

At last he put the flogger down and released me from my restraints. My body was weak and I fell into his arms. He untied the rope and gently laid me on a sheepskin rug and when he did I noticed his erection. At first I felt it and without thinking about what I was doing, I reached out to touch it and found myself rubbing him through his jeans.

I could feel it growing harder so I began to undo the buttons, so that I could free his erection. Despite all that he had done to me, I still wanted him. Plus I knew that if I was going to come out of this thing alive, I was going to have to get him to trust me and that meant showing him that I wanted him just as much as he wanted me.

I moaned and my body strained upwards towards his as Devlin dipped his head, and caught one nipple between his teeth and bit down, while twisting the other between his fingers.

"Does that feel good?"

"Yes, Master." It really didn't feel good, it hurt like hell, but I knew what he wanted me to say.

I was finally able to unfastened his jeans and free his cock. As I stroked my hand up and down his length, he let out a low groan. It was sexy sounding, almost primal. I was sore from the beating I had taken, but still found myself getting wet for him.

I put my hand under his shirt and ran it up his hard stomach. He did have an amazing body and I wanted to see more of it. I tugged at the bottom of his shirt, trying to get him to remove it and finally he sat up, and pulled it up over his head, giving me what I wanted. I couldn't help myself, I just had to run my tongue up and down the ridges of his well-toned abs.

So far he was letting me get away with my aggressive sexual behavior and I wondered just how far I could push it. My hand reached up to cup his cheek and I kissed him softly, pushing our bodies closer together and when I did, his hard cock strained against my stomach. It felt good and made me want him even more. With my other hand I reached down and started to stroke his cock again. It was huge and hard and ready for me.

He gently ran a finger down the side of my face, from my hairline to my jaw, tracing along my cheekbone. I gazed up at him, taking in his beautiful blue eyes. He ran his fingers gently over my lips and then pressed his mouth to mine.

He kissed me passionately while I slowly stroked his cock. Pulling back he looked into my eyes, perhaps trying to judge my sincerity. I'm not sure, what it was he was looking for but suddenly a smirk came across his face.

"You seem to enjoy touching that, don't you?"

"Yes, I do. May I kiss it Master?"

He didn't answer me. He just pushed my head down gently, letting me have my way. I took his head into my mouth, then worked my tongue up and down his shaft. I could tell his breathing was getting heavier and I knew that meant he liked it.

I tilted my head back so I could look up at him again and then opened my mouth wide, letting him see my lips cover the head of his cock. I tossed my hair over my shoulder and then took him deep into my mouth and he let out a guttural groan.

I slowly slid my lips further along his shaft, taking him in deeper while I gently began playing with his balls. I pulled back, stopping only when the head was just about to pop out of my mouth and then took him all the way in again, swirling my tongue around his length. I looked back up and him and noticed his eyes were closed and his breath was coming in slow pants.

I couldn't help but smile around the head of his cock. I liked knowing that I had that effect on him. I squeezed one hand tightly around the base of his cock while with the other I continued to play with his balls. When I did he grunted and his cock started to twitch. As I bobbed my head up and down, he pushed my face down onto his cock, thrusting his hips forward.

It was all so arousing a low moan escape my lips and I could feel how wet I was. I wanted to reach between my thighs and play with my pussy, but I remembered what happened the night before when I did and instead did my best to restrain my desires.

Suddenly he jerked my head back and pulled his cock out of my mouth. He stood up and roughly jerked me up, lifting me up, off of the ground. I wrapped my legs around his waist, assuming he was going to carry me to the bedroom and have his way with me but he didn't. Instead he cupped my ass with both hands and lifted me up and then slammed me down onto his cock. He filled every inch of me and it felt incredible. He was big, big enough that it stretched me out completely. It took a moment for my body to adjust to his size.

I couldn't believe we were standing up having sex. Just the thought of how strong he must be to not only carry me but continue to lift me, forcing me up and down on his cock was even more of a turn on.

I admit my experience in the bedroom is a little lacking, but if I knew it could be like this, I would have tried to have it far more often. This was incredible. I never even imagined sex in a position like that was possible and yet here we were doing it. I have had sex before, but it was absolutely never like this.

I was so taken away by what he was doing to me, I let out a low moan from deep within my chest. I'd never done that before. I've moaned and groaned before, but this was different, like someone else or something else was taking over my body.

"God, you are so fucking tight," he groaned.

I didn't respond. I didn't want him to know the truth that I hadn't been with many men before. By the time most girls are twenty-one they had been with countless men. But I wasn't that way, I was always so shy.

Using his strong arms he continued to lift me up and slam me down on his cock again and again. My breath quickened as his hard cock pumped inside of me. I closed my eyes, doing my best to stop myself from coming.

"You want to come for me don't you?"

"Yes, Master," I barely got out. I was losing control and fast.

"That's a good girl, come for me."

I pushed my ass back to meet his thrusts, and as I did I felt him explode inside of me, just as my own orgasm ripped through me. It left me shuddering, unable to breathe and I held on to his body tightly. As I was holding on for dear life, he held me securely in place until I was done. His cock still pulsing and throbbing inside of me.

He carried me to the bedroom and put me down on the bed. He didn't lay down next to me like I thought he might. Instead he stood over me, securing my wrist to the bedframe again with the handcuffs.

He went to get me a bottle of water, helped me drink it and when I was finished he leaned down and kissed my forehead.

"Get some rest, my slave. I'll come check on you later."

I didn't respond. I just closed my eyes and did as he told me to.

Chapter 7

I awoke to see him standing over me, fully dressed in a suit and tie. I knew instantly that it was a work day and that I should be leaving soon for the office. Yet here I was, a prisoner, completely naked in this man's penthouse, and my entire body ached.

"Good morning my slave. I hope you slept well."

He stroked my hair, which must have been looking unkempt by now. I couldn't believe I actually slept through the whole night.

"Would you like to use the bathroom?"

"Yes please Master, I would."

He undid the handcuffs and I slipped down from the bed onto my hands and knees.

"You may use the pink toothbrush. I bought it especially for you."

I crawled towards the bathroom and felt a sting from his crop.

"We don't have all morning you know."

"Yes, Master."

I crawled into the bathroom and shut the door, hoping he would not walk in on me today. It seemed I was to be lucky this morning and I used the toilet and started the shower running without interruption. I looked by the sink and there, as promised, was a pink toothbrush in a glass. There was toothpaste too and mouthwash. I brushed my teeth and rinsed with the mouthwash and immediately felt better.

The shower felt good on my bruised body and I soaped myself from head to toe before washing my hair. After I turned off the water and stepped out of the shower. I wrapped a towel around my body. It felt strange to have something, even a towel, covering my body after the last few days of being naked.

I noticed the razor and remembered his instructions to shave every day. I took off the towel and sat on the little stool, lifting my leg up to rest on the edge of the bath. I thoroughly shaved myself. I noticed there was a hairdryer in the bathroom, together with various brushes and combs. They all looked brand new. I dried and combed my hair, trying my best to hurry, not wanting to keep him waiting. Then after taking a look at myself in the mirror, I crawled out of the bathroom.

"You took rather a long time in there."

He pulled the towel off from around my body and then I felt the sharp sting of the crop across my ass.

"I'm sorry, Master."

He brought the crop down hard once more across my thighs.

"I will forgive you this time."

"Thank you Master."

"Now get back on the bed."

I did as I was told and he again handcuffed me to the bed frame.

"Time for breakfast."

He went into the kitchen and returned with a tray loaded with coffee, croissants, toast and strawberries. Like before, he fed me my breakfast. It was strange having someone feed me, but on the other hand it was also kind of nice the way he looked after me.

He fed me little pieces of toast smothered in grape jelly and pieces of a croissant, buttered to perfection. He also fed me strawberries dipped in sugar. I was very hungry and ate everything he offered me.

He held out a coffee cup. "Cream, no sugar."

He smiled as I took it with my free hand.

"I have a very special afternoon planned."

"Yes Master, what is it?"

"You will find out in good time. For now have some more strawberries."

"Thank you Master."

He dipped a strawberry into the sugar and held it up to my lips. I parted them and took a big bite out of the fruit. Finally I was sated and he wiped my mouth.

'Thank you Master. It was a wonderful breakfast."

"I have to go out for a while but I have something special planned for this afternoon so get some rest, I want you fresh."

I wasn't tired, I had only just woken up from a full night's rest but he left me no choice. I was handcuffed to the bed and couldn't exactly do anything until he released me from my bonds. I was bored out of my mind while he was away. I continued to run the memory of entering the building through my mind to see if I could find something I might have missed. I still hadn't found the fire escape but I also hadn't had much of a chance to look.

I decided that when Devlin returned I would ask him if I could have a book to read in his absence. I couldn't just lay here in bed and stare mindlessly at the ceiling all day, every day, while he was at work or running errands, I would go out of my mind.

I wondered what he had planned for this afternoon. I had never been good with surprises and the thought of what we could be doing rushed through my mind. I made myself as comfortable as I could and closed my eyes. Perhaps he was going to take me home. My mind was in a whirl. I don't know how long he was away it could have been minutes or hours, but I eventually heard his key in the lock. He came into the bedroom carrying a bag which he put down in a corner of the room.

I was burning with curiosity, "Please Master what do you have planned?"

"All in good time but first we have to get you dressed."

I was delighted at the prospect of wearing clothes again and could hardly contain myself. He picked up the bag from the floor and placed it on the bed. He undid the handcuffs and I sat up straight.

"I hope you like what I chose for you my sweet slave."

I looked and saw a loose fitting, little black dress and a pair of black pumps, with a matching set of black lace bra and panties. It was simple, yet elegant.

"Thank you Master for getting these things for me to wear."

I dressed as quickly as I could. My body was sore from the beatings I had taken and my clothes rubbed painfully against my skin but I was keen to get going.

"Ok," he smiled "just go and brush your hair before we go."

I hurried into the bathroom to make myself presentable. When I left the bathroom I could barely contain my excitement. I was ready to go back out in the world again after being held captive in his apartment for days. Maybe I would get an opportunity to escape.

"You look lovely my slave. There is just one thing missing." He held up a leash which he fastened to my collar. "Now you are ready to go out."

I was horrified and couldn't believe that he expected me to go out wearing a leash like he was walking his dog. However it was clear that he did and there was little I could do about it. It was go out like this or not go at all.

"Are you ready?"

I nodded and he headed towards the front door with me following behind him. We left the apartment and took the elevator down to the ground floor. I paid close attention to every detail, hoping to find something, anything I could use in my escape plan later on.

As we walked to the parking garage, I was grateful there weren't many people outside. The few that passed us averted their eyes or laughed quietly. I flushed crimson with embarrassment but was grateful we had only been seen by a few people. It could have been much worse.

When we got to his car he opened the door for me like a gentleman. As I sat down, he leaned over me and fastened my seatbelt. It was the little things like that, which confused me most. In some ways he has taken such good care of me, yet I'm still held prisoner, against my will.

We didn't drive for long before arriving at our destination. After opening the door for me to get out of the car, he took a tight hold on my leash and had to pull me to get me to leave the car.

Reluctantly I got out of the car dreading every step I took. The people that passed us weren't as polite as the others and there was quite a bit of pointing and laughing as I was led down the street. I'd never been so humiliated in my life.

We walked past several store fronts in the shopping center. Finally we came upon a tattoo parlor with people hanging around outside it. He firmly pulled on my leash and led me past them. There were catcalls and whistles. I tried to ignore them but it wasn't easy.

He pushed through the people blocking the door and entered the place. I could hear the buzzing of needles and the shop was covered from floor to ceiling with tattoo designs. He headed up a flight of stairs with me following behind. It was not so crowded upstairs. He knocked on a door and it was opened by a heavily tattooed man. The two seemed to know each other and exchanged warm greetings. We stepped into the room and the door closed behind us. I was told to kneel and I obeyed, wondering what we were doing here.

Devlin and his friend talked for a while but I could not hear what they were saying. Then the man came over to me, ordered me to stand and ran his hand over my breasts.

"She has lovely tits, have you thought about nipple rings?"

"Not today," Devlin replied. "Just what we discussed on the phone."

I began to get nervous. What could they be talking about? What did Devlin plan on having this man do to me?

"Come over here," Devlin ordered and I did as I was told.

Tugging at my leash he led me over to what looked like a dentist's chair. As I took my seat in the chair he unclipped my leash from my collar.

"What's going on Master?"

"I'm going to mark you as my slave, a permanent tattoo which will be with you for the rest of your life."

The tattoo artist took his spot and began to run his fingers over my skin. He ran his hand slowly up and down my arm.

"She's a pretty girl. Her skin is soft, near perfection." He leaned over and sniffed me. "She smells good too."

I was scared now, really scared. This man was beyond creepy. Why was Devlin allowing this man to touch me like this?

"Oh what I would do to you if you were mine," he said quietly as he continued to run his hands over my body in a most disturbing way.

"Please, I don't want to do this," I cried. "Please. I'm scared."

"Sssh," Devlin soothed. "It's going to be alright."

Devlin stood at the foot of the dentist's chair and forced my legs apart which pushed my skirt up, exposing my lace panties. The tattoo artist who was sitting on a stool with wheels, rolled down towards my feet to get a better look.

I couldn't believe Devlin was showing this man I don't even know my panties.

"Pull then aside," Devlin ordered.

I hesitated but he gave me a look and I knew I had no choice. If I didn't comply I would pay dearly for it later. I scooted down just a bit, forcing my dress up even more, where it was now around my waist and I hesitantly put my hands between my legs, pulling my panties aside, exposing my pussy.

"Well, well what do we have here?" The tattoo artist said while greedily looking at me. "May I?" He asked Devlin and surprisingly Devlin nodded in approval.

The tattoo artist inserted a finger into my pussy while Devlin watched on. As the man worked his finger in and out of my pussy, I found my body reacting and could feel myself starting to get wet. When I let out a soft moan, Devlin finally put a stop to it.

"I think that is enough for now."

The tattooist reluctantly withdrew his fingers and pulled away from me.

"Let's get on with what we came for," Devlin commanded.

Immediately professional, the tattooist asked if he had decided on a design yet. Devlin pulled a piece of paper out of his pocket with a roughly sketched out design. It was the word 'forever' in a beautiful cursive script. The man started to draw the design and I began to protest.

"No Master, please," I begged.

"Be quiet or you will be punished."

I did as I was told and sat there quietly while the stranger went and disinfected his hands, and then carefully wiped my wrist with antiseptic.

"I will need your help," he said to Devlin. "Hold her very still."

"That's perfect" he said as the transfer went on my skin.

"Now just hold her still while I do this."

I heard the buzzing of the needle and braced myself for the pain. It was intense and the process seemed to go on forever. I thought they would never stop. My wrist was on fire.

Tears were pouring down my face, but that didn't seem to matter, because they just kept going, permanently marking my body, forever branding me as his.

Eventually he stopped and invited Devlin to have a look at his work.

"Very nice, very nice indeed."

I didn't look. But it wouldn't have mattered. My eyes were swollen from crying so I wouldn't have been able to see it anyway.

Devlin paid the man and I was glad to finally get out of there. He clipped my leash back on my collar and we left the room. It was even more crowded downstairs than when we first arrived and I could hear the jeers and whistles ringing in my ears. But I didn't pay them any mind, I just wanted to get out of there.

Getting a tattoo freaking hurts. Why are they so popular? What the hell is wrong with people to willingly agree to put themselves through such pain?

I remembered little of the drive back to his penthouse, mostly I was just focused on the pain. I was glad when we got back to Devlin's place. Once we stepped off the elevated and into his foyer he carried me into the bedroom, removed my clothes and laid me down on the bed.

"You've done well. I'm pleased with you."

He held me against his body and played with my hair as I fell asleep in the safety and security of his arms.

Chapter 8

It was dark when I woke up and I was alone with my thoughts. Time was beginning to become meaningless, and I had no idea if it was day or night, nor did I care. Why did it matter? It wouldn't make me any less of his slave.

I let my mind drift to what my days used to be like. I thought about what I used to do each day at work and I could almost smell the coffee I would have each morning at my desk, when I first got into the office.

My mind began to wander from the life I used to have to what happened earlier. There was a burning sensation from the tattoo. I can't believe he branded me like I was his property. It was still bandaged but I didn't need to see the ink on my wrist to remember what happened.

I heard Devlin in the kitchen and realized I wasn't handcuffed to the bed. This was the first time I had woke up untethered. I thought about trying to make a run for it, but quickly put that thought out of my head. I wouldn't make it to the front door before he caught me and I still hadn't figured out where the stupid fire escape even was, if there even was one. Surely there had to be one. Don't all hi-rise buildings have to have them?

The more I thought about everything, the angrier I became. This tattoo was the final straw. I decided that

I'd had enough and went into the kitchen to confront him.

"I'm not doing this anymore Devlin."

He leaned against the counter and smirked.

"You've kidnapped me, held me hostage, refused to let me wear clothes, beat me repeatedly, made me crawl around on all fours like I was an animal and you won't even let me go potty with the bathroom door locked and now you've marred my body with this tattoo."

I lifted my wrist and pointed to the bandage.

"What are you going to do next, get out a cattle iron and brand my ass?"

He didn't respond. He just kept looking at me with that smirk on his face.

"I can't even sleep like a normal person at night because you insist on handcuffing me to the bed. I'm not doing this anymore. I've had enough. I want to go home. You've had your fun but enough is enough. I'm not your pet. I'm a human being and I have rights. You can't treat me like this."

He just kept grinning at me and let me continue on with my rant. He didn't even appear to be angry with me, seeming almost amused by my outburst.

"Well, say something!" I demanded.

"Aren't we feeling a little spunky today?"

"If you think I'm going to answer you 'Yes, Master' you've lost your mind. I'm done with all of that. I want to go home Devlin. I'm serious. Take me home right this minute!"

I turned with my back to him, not wanting to let him see me tear up. And then I felt him. He came up behind me and a sensation unlike any I had felt before tore through me. I couldn't feel him but I knew he was near me. The pull was beyond my control.

There was something delusional about these thoughts I kept having about him. This man is forcing my sanity to fly out the window and I couldn't for the life of me explain why. I enjoyed being the focus of his attention, and I enjoyed the way he took care of me yet at the same time, I knew that was wrong. I knew I shouldn't care anything about this man. This is my abductor, not a potential husband.

Being around Devlin had a strange effect on me, and I couldn't understand it. I mean yes he was a beautiful man -- that goes without saying, but I had been around attractive men before. It's not like I lived in a cave all of my life. But this was more and I couldn't quite put my finger on what it was about him that was beyond the normal realm of appealing. Why was I so drawn to him even after the way he has treated me?

For the last year, any time he was anywhere near me my brain would just shut down and my body would tingle with desire. A year of this unexplainable pull towards him, to have it all end up like this?

I remembered his touch, and a chill ran up my spine. How crazy am I to get turned on just by the memory of him touching me? What is wrong with me? God, I even loved the way he woke me up each morning, with his deep masculine voice. I really did love the way he said "Good morning." Then again, I loved the way he said most things. His voice alone could drive me over the edge.

"Are you finished?" he murmured from behind me.

I froze. His words hit me like a slap to the face. Am I finished? Seriously? That's all he had to say to me?

"Why are you doing this to me?" I asked, as I turned to face him.

He didn't answer my question. Instead he took me by the hand and led me into a room I hadn't seen before. He drenched my body in baby oil, taking his time to rub it in thoroughly, making my skin slick.

"This will help you not to get rope burns."

I didn't know what he meant but it felt so good having his hands all over my body, I didn't stop to give it much thought.

When he was done rubbing the baby oil in, he had me straddle a chair and then secured my legs far apart, keeping them in place with a thick rope. He handcuffed my hands behind my back and then put a ball gag in my mouth.

Now it didn't matter what he did to me, because I couldn't move or scream for help. I was scared. Maybe I shouldn't have had my little outburst after all.

"Your life is no longer your own. Your body belongs to me. I told you on that first day here, my word is law. You are my property, my slave. You will learn to obey me. You will learn to submit."

He smacked my upper thigh with a leather riding crop. It stung. He hit my other thigh, then my stomach, each of my breasts and then my pussy. The pain from that stroke was unimaginable. I cried out but the ball gag prevented any sound from being heard. Luckily he didn't hit my pussy but the one time. The other strokes were focused mostly on my upper thighs and stomach, with each of my breasts getting struck a few times as well.

I don't know how long this went on, it could have been twenty strokes or two hundred. All I knew for sure was that my body was bright red and swollen from being struck repeatedly with the riding crop.

I knew what he was doing. He was breaking me down so that he could build me back up. I got it. The military does the same thing. That's what basic training was all about. But even knowing what he was doing, didn't make the pain he inflicted any easier to bare.

The red slashes and welts covered practically all of my body. I began to grow woozy and started to pass out from the pain. It was all just too much to take. I couldn't handle it anymore.

When I woke up I was handcuffed to the bed again, alone in the dark. Tears began streaming down my cheeks, my voice quaking in terror, as I let out a pitiful cry.

My body ached from the lashes that had bitten into my bare flesh and I was feeling sick to my stomach, I felt like I might throw up but I couldn't move. If I was going to get sick, I would have to lay there in it for God only knows how long, until he came in to check on me and let me clean myself up. If he let me clean myself up. He was a sadistic bastard, for all I knew, he would make me lay in my own vomit to punish me for getting sick in the first place.

I did my best to keep from throwing up and eventually, when I stopped crying he came into the bedroom. He released me from the cuffs and helped me sit up and gently brushed the hair out of my eyes.

With him he had a bowl of ice cold water and some strips of linen which he dipped into the freezing water and lightly placed on my skin. The coolness of the cloth felt good and helped to sooth the welts on my body. I laid perfectly still as he cared for my wounds.

"That's a good girl," he soothed.

While he was caring for me, I must have fallen back asleep. I don't know how long I was out but when I woke up I could see the sun shining through the window and knew it was a new day.

I could smell the scent of fresh bacon and heard my stomach growl and soon after Devlin entered the room with a tray in hand. For breakfast today he made scrambled eggs, bacon, toast with strawberry jelly and a glass of orange juice.

I tried to use my one free hand to prop myself up, but it hurt too much to move. I grimaced and he rushed to my side, setting the tray of food down and removed my handcuffs.

"Good morning," he said as he helped me sit all the way up.

"I need to go to the restroom. Do you think you can help me get up?"

He gave me a stern look. "Please Master, I don't think I can get out of bed without your help."

He smiled down at me and gently helped me get out of bed. As soon as I stood up I fell to the floor. The pain was so intense, I couldn't stand up on my own. He picked me up off of the floor and carried me to the bathroom, sitting me down on the toilet. I was humiliated at having him there while I relieved myself but what else could I do? I couldn't walk without him. After I finished he helped me wash my hands and face and then carried me back to bed and fed me breakfast.

He was so tender and loving with me and for just a moment it was easy to imagine having a great life with him. That is, this version of him. I liked him liked this. I liked having him lavish me with affection and attention. This was the Devlin that I was first attracted to. He had a sensitive loving heart and lively spirit that drew everyone to him. If only this Devlin would stay around all the time.

After breakfast Devlin ran me a warm bath that he had filled with Epsom salt to help my wounds heal and the swelling go down. When we were done he carried me back to bed and rubbed scented oils into my body. It was relaxing and before long I was asleep yet again. I had read once that when you are not feeling well your body uses sleep to help recover. As much as I was sleeping lately, I supposed my body's recovery system must have been in hyper-drive.

After a few days of extensive bed rest and tender, loving care from Devlin I finally started to feel almost human again. Devlin informed me that he had to go into work for a few hours. I felt almost panicked at hearing that he would be leaving me alone and it must have shown on my face.

"It's okay," he said soothingly as he patted my leg. "I'll be back before you know it. Do you want to watch some television while I am away?"

"I would. Thank you Master."

This was the first time he was going to trust me out of bed while he was away. There wouldn't however be a chance for me to escape because he secured me to a chair in the living room. I had one hand free but one hand and both legs were chained.

I flipped mindlessly through the channels until I happened upon a re-run of one of the Twilight movies. I've seen them all before, several times before, but nothing else was on so I watched it again.

When the movie ended I started flipping channels again and happened upon a skin flick, one of the 'Cinemax After Dark' type movies about two girls who were in love with the same guy but decided to get back at him for cheating on them both by dating each other.

Caught up in the show, I didn't hear the noise of the door opening before it was too late and Devlin entered the penthouse.

"Well, well. What do we have here?" He asked, as he came in and looked at what was on the television.

I scrambled to turn it off but it was too late. He had already seen what was on the screen.

"It's not what you think."

"What is it then? Are you telling me you don't have some secret desire to be with another girl?"

"No!" I said in protest. I could feel my face glowing bright red and turned away from him. I couldn't let him see just how embarrassed I was over all of this.

"What is it then?"

He sat down next to me and ran his hand up and down my thighs, caressing me.

"It's their clothes," I admitted reluctantly.

He looked at me in confusion. "Were we not watching the same movie? Those girls didn't have much on in the way of clothes."

"Of course they did. They had on sexy lingerie and thigh high stockings with fancy jewelry and ..."

"Okay I get it. You are trying to say that you would like something more to wear around the house?"

"Well yeah. But it's not just about wearing clothes. It's about looking sexy. They didn't just have on clothes. They had on intimate attire. I never really had anything like that before. They were all sexy, but at the same time so feminine. Know what I mean?"

He let out a soft chuckle. "I do. But you'll have to go with me to buy it. You have a tiny little body and for something like this, it will need to be fitted."

"Really?" I said excitedly.

"Yes, I'm sure we can buy you a few new things to wear."

He kissed my forehead and started to pull back but I grabbed him with my one free hand and pulled him in for a real kiss.

I licked his lips and began kissing down his collarbone, pulling back the collar of his shirt to get to bare skin. Forgetting about my restraints, I tried to put my arms around his neck and got a quick reminder.

I looked up at him with pleading eyes. He pulled the key out of his pocket and freed both my hands and feet. I thanked him with another kiss on his lips, this time more passionate while using my hands to unbutton his shirt.

He pulled back, looking at me through heavy lidded eyes. He made no effort to stop me so I continued removing his clothes. After I sat up on my knees and pushed my breasts into his face. It felt so good to lean my naked body against his bare chest, to rub up against his muscled body. But it felt even better to have his mouth on my breasts.

He grabbed my face, pulling me down to him. He paused for just a moment, looking at me and then he kissed me. He stood up and took me by the hand, clearly intending to lead me somewhere but then he stopped. Instead he ran his hands over my ass in a soft caress and then slid a finger inside of me. I was writhing under his touch, practically humping his hand.

I was panting, wanting more from him and about two seconds from coming when he pulled his fingers out of me. I looked up at him with a pout on my face.

"Come with me," he said.

I followed him to the bedroom.

"Lay on your stomach," he commanded.

He opened one of the drawers and pulled something out, but I couldn't see what it was. He leaned over me, and put a pillow under my stomach so that my ass was now in the air. I froze, unsure what was going to happen next.

He ran his hands over my back side, down the split of my ass, teasing me, making me want him even more. He squirted something cold on my ass and began to massage it in. I squirmed but he was sitting on top of me, holding me in place.

"Don't tense up."

With one hand he started to play with my clit and it felt great. I quickly forgot about what he was doing with his other hand. That was until he inserted something in my ass.

I squeaked. "What is that?"

"It's a butt plug. Don't worry I used the smallest one. We need to start training that cute little ass of yours."

Before I could protest he started rubbing my clit faster and I lost my train of thought. The more he teased my clit the more I got used to what he stuck in my ass and quite honestly it started to feel good. It was a strange sensation, something I wasn't used to, but I liked it. Somehow it made what he was doing to my pussy feel even better and I wanted more. I was so turned on.

"I want you to fuck me Master," I said as I was thrusting my hips back and forth, grinding against his hand.

"Please Master, I need you inside of me."

I didn't have to wait for long before he lifted my ass up in the air and rammed his cock in my pussy.

Even though I was wet and desperately wanted him inside of me, it was still a tight fit at first and it took a moment for my body to adjust. With each stroke though it began to feel better and I soon started thrusting my hips to meet his strokes.

"God your pussy is so tight you are killing me."

I knew he was speaking to me but I could barely hear his words. All I could do is feel the immense pleasure of him thrusting in and out of me. I reached between my legs and started rubbing my clit. When I did his thrusts grew harder, and faster. As good as the slow, deep strokes had felt I enjoyed the change of pace, relishing the power emanating from his muscular body.

As he drove his cock impossibly deep into me I felt possessed by him, it was as if each stroke pounded through my very being. I knew I couldn't hold out much longer, the sense of pleasure was just too great.

"I'm going to come in that sweet little pussy of yours."

I began to writhe beneath him, desperate for satisfaction when finally my orgasm took over my body and filled me with an intense gratification. I could feel my juices running down the shaft of his cock. Devlin put his finger against my opening and coaxed out a little juice and then put it up to his lips.

"You taste so fucking good."

My clit quivered and pulsed with aftershocks and he started fucking me again. I could tell he was struggling not to come but my pussy was swollen and stretched so tight around his cock. His hands clenched desperately at my waist, as he buried himself repeatedly inside of me. It was flesh against flesh and the only sound that echoed through the room was the harsh slap of his bodying meeting mine and the soft grunts that escaped his lips.

Turning me over, he looked down at me with a supreme satisfaction written all over his face.

"You're so beautiful," he said tenderly.

He slid a finger inside of my pussy that was now full of his hot seed. Then he traced a line around my mouth. I slowly ran my tongue over my lips, tasting his semen.

"Good girl," he said as he smiled down at me.

He rolled over, lying next to me, pulling me into his arms. Resting my head on his chest, the sound of his heartbeat put me to sleep. I'm not sure how long I was out but when I woke up my hand was resting on his cock and it was hard yet again.

He was still sleeping and I didn't want to wake him so I decided to satisfy myself. I slid my hand between my legs. My flesh was still slick with him come from earlier so my fingers moved easily through my folds.

I tried my best to be quiet but it wasn't easy. I wanted to come badly I began to make tiny moans without realizing it and that woke Devlin up. He turned on his side and propped himself up on his elbow to watch.

"Don't let me stop you," he said mischievously.

I pulled my fingers out of my pussy, embarrassed that I had been caught.

"I want to watch," he said as he guided my hand back down to my pussy.

I rolled my middle finger over my clit, moaning softly as my entire body tightened. I found my sweet spot and rubbed it vigorously as my pussy pulsed and clenched in response.

I arched my back and worked my finger faster over my clit. He leaned down and bit my nipple and I cried out in pain, but didn't stop. It was a delicious pain and only made me even more turned on.

My breathing rose sharply and my body was wound up like a rubber band. I needed release and stroked faster. My hand moved in a frenzy and my hips rose and fell as I worked my finger in and out of my pussy until finally, in one sudden burst I catapulted over the edge and my orgasm shook me.

I had never played with myself in front of anyone before. How was this man able to get me to do such things? The old me would have never considered doing something like that before. But with Devlin I barely gave it a second thought. Knowing he was watching me pleasure myself made it even more stimulating.

Chapter 9

We went to shower together and after he had me fix my hair and put on clothes.

"Where are we going Master?"

"You don't need to worry about that right now."

I was dying of curiosity but held my tongue. I knew he would tell me when he was ready and if I annoyed him by asking too many questions, I risked further punishment and that was the last thing I wanted.

I put on the summer dress he set out for me, along with the matching bra and panties. Just as I slipped on my shoes he attached the leash to my collar.

"Ok, let's go".

I followed after him as he let us out of the penthouse.

We took the elevator down to the ground floor and went out of the main door into the sunshine. Fortunately, there were few people around so I was not subjected to stares. When we got into the car I couldn't help but ask again where we were headed.

"We are going shopping for something for you to wear. We are going to the club tonight and I want you to look your best."

A hundred questions whirled round in my mind. What club? Did he mean the bar by the office that we went to on the first Friday of every month or did he mean somewhere else? Who would be there? Would there be a chance for me to escape?

There were too many questions for me to cope with at the moment, so I put them out of my mind and instead focused on the present. We were going out and we were going shopping for clothes. I welcomed the chance to get out of his penthouse and was even more excited to be getting something new to wear.

We drove across town. I recognized the area, it was not too far from where I lived. When I saw the shopping mall off in the distance I began to get worried that he intended to parade me around on the leash. As we drove passed the mall entrance, I turned to look at him, wondering where in the world we were headed. He didn't answer, instead just kept driving.

We eventually pulled into a parking lot of a building I didn't recognize. With a name like Forbidden Pleasures, I knew what kind of place it must have been. We parked in the back and he came around to open my door like a gentleman and then led me into the store by my leash.

Unlike last time, there weren't a lot of stares and jeers. The people in this store acted as if they were used to seeing men lead women around on a leash. When we got to the door, it was locked. We had to ring the bell to be let in. He exchanged warm greetings with the man who let us in as if he knew him well.

The store was rather large and had all sorts of leather and rubber garments. There were also peephole bras, crotchless panties, corsets and fishnet stockings.

Devlin turned to me and told me to strip except for my bra and panties. I was frozen to the spot. Strip in front of all these strangers? I couldn't make my arms and legs move.

"Strip or this goes into the punishment book."

At the mention of the book I reluctantly removed my clothes. I would rather be standing in front of all of these people naked than to get punished again.

I felt several pairs of eyes boring into me and looked up at Devlin pleadingly. He chose to ignore my look. So there I was, naked in front of these people I didn't know, completely horrified.

"She's pretty" said one of the customers, who wouldn't stop staring at my breasts, which were barely contained in my lace, push up bra.

I looked over at Devlin, who seemed quite happy for the man to be lusting after me. Luckily the saleswoman came over and sent the man away as she took me by the hand and led me over to a selection of dresses she thought I might like.

The first thing she showed me was a sequin one sleeve dress. Devlin wouldn't let me out of his sight so he accompanied me and the sales associate to the dressing room where I tried it on. The dress was a perfect fit and he nodded his approval and then instructed her to show us more. She brought over a bejeweled jumpsuit that I fell in love with but Devlin didn't agree.

"No. Absolutely not. No jeans, no pants, no shorts. How you look is a direct reflection on me."

He had a grim look on his face so I decided not to push the issue. If he didn't want me wearing pants I could live with that.

The next dress she brought me to try on left me completely speechless. It was elegant and sexy and when I put it on, I had never felt as sexy in my life. The dress was red and backless, and the front was extremely low cut, with an opening all the way down to expose below my belly button.

"Do you have that in black?" Devlin asked the lady.

"Yes, we do."

"Great. We'll take it in black."

Next she brought in a white corset and a matching white tutu. I felt so pretty and pranced around to show it off for Devlin. He seemed amused and agreed to buy the outfit in all white, all black and a version that was a combination of black and white.

I thought carefully about each of my purchases, knowing that whatever I selected, no matter how sexy or see through, he could make me wear in public. So I was careful to only select dresses that covered all of my private parts.

In between trying on outfits another employee of the store served us champagne. A few drinks in I began to feel a little frisky and instead of taking the seat next to Devlin while I waited for the lady to bring me her next suggested selection, I sat on his lap.

As she brought the next dress to me, I looked at her closely. She was pretty, really pretty and tall with a great tan with wonderfully long legs. She could have easily been mistaken for a Victoria Secret's model. She was thin and had very tiny breasts. I began to wonder what they felt like and I found myself wanting to lick them.

Obviously it wasn't just me because with each new dress, she got more intimate with her touches. There was definitely a spark between us.

"You like her, don't you?" Devlin whispered in my ear.

I nodded in agreement, while watching her walk towards us.

"She has you wet, doesn't she?"

I didn't get a chance to respond before he put a finger inside me, just enough to feel how wet I was.

"That's what I thought."

"I'm sorry Master. I don't know what has come over me. She's just so ... tall."

"It's okay. I don't mind you playing with other girls."

I looked at him in surprise. "Really?"

"Of course. As long as you ask my permission, I don't mind."

"I've never done that before. I wouldn't know what to even do Master."

"Just touch her how you would want her to touch you."

That totally made sense. I guess I could do that. I quickly downed the rest of my glass of champagne and when she came back over with a short silver mini-skirt for me to try on, I decided to try and make a move.

"Now this outfit has some matching silver go-go boots and a plunging top that ties up front. You won't be able to wear a bra with the top though," she explained to me while helping me adjust the teeny tiny metallic skirt around my hips.

I removed my bra and as she stood up her lips grazed my nipple. She gave me her sexist smile while removing her top. I unhooked her black bra, slid it off and threw it over my shoulder, landing on Devlin.

She let her hair down and it cascaded down her shoulders to stop just at the top of her perky little tits. She pulled me in for one of those long, movie-type kisses and then traced a line with her finger from the top of my panties down to the middle. I knew she could feel my wetness, even through the fabric. She pulled my panties aside and stuck her finger deep inside of me as I squealed with desire.

I opened my legs wider for her touch and when I did she stuck two fingers inside of me. Her fingers created a rhythm in my slippery wetness and I was helpless to do anything but moan.

Her touch was soft and pleasurable. I felt my clit began to throb and knew I wasn't too far off from reaching a state of pure ecstasy but before we could go any further, the store owner stepped into the dressing room and found me making out with his sales associate.

"Imogen, what did I tell you about sleeping with the clientele?"

Imogen rushed to get her clothes back on and I pulled the skirt down that I was trying on.

"I'm sorry boss," the sales associate said as she lowered her head and went back to selecting outfits for me to try on.

"Don't be too hard on her Martin. She's been making you a lot of money this afternoon."

Devlin pointed to the stack of dresses we already picked out to buy. The store owner turned his attention from the girl to Devlin.

"Devlin, old pal, what have you been up to? It's been ages since we've seen you around here."

"Yes indeed it has. But as you can see I've been making up for lost time."

Imogen returned with several more outfit selections including a dress of vinyl and one made out of latex.

I wasn't a big fan of the latex dress so I sent that back but I did keep the one made out of vinyl. It wasn't as complicated as the latex one was to put on.

As I was taking off the last dress something else caught my attention. It was a glittery, wide rhinestone choker that spelled out SLAVE, in big bold letters. I loved it and had to have it.

As she put it around my neck, Imogen explained that it was made of sterling silver and Swarovski crystals.

It fit perfectly over my black leather slave collar. I turned to Devlin with pleading eyes and a huge smile crossed his lips. He gestured for me to come to him and he examined it more carefully.

"Is this something you really want?"

"Oh yes Master, I absolutely love it. It will go perfect with the black low cut dress from earlier. I thought maybe if it was okay with you that is what I would wear tonight."

He lovingly ran his hand down the side of my face. "Okay my sweet, you can have it."

Devlin continued to talk to the store owner while Imogen fitted me with several pair of shoes to match the outfits I had selected. Next we picked out some bra and pantie sets and a large selection of thigh high stockings of various colors and designs.

I've never been one of those girls with a shoe fetish, but looking at all of the great heels that Devlin bought me, I can totally see how some girls are so obsessed with them. I can't wait to wear them. I especially can't wait to wear the black Christian Louboutin pumps with little black spikes coming out of them. I also got a pair of open toe Badgley Mischka heels. Overall I think I ended up getting about ten different pair of shoes. I don't know where I am going to wear them to but one thing's for sure, I can't wait to have an excuse to wear those scarlet red glitter platform pumps. Who knows, I may just walk around the house naked in them.

I got dressed as Devlin paid for my new clothes. After he reconnected my leash and walked me to the car while several of the store employees carried our bags, loading them up in the trunk of Devlin's car.

On the way home he was quiet and I was lost in my own thoughts. It wasn't until we pulled up outside the building of his penthouse, that I even realized we didn't say a single word to each other the entire drive. He helped me out of the car and immediately turned to start walking the short distance to the front door. Before going in I grabbed his hand to get his attention.

"Is everything okay, Master?"

"Yes my sweet. I just have a lot on my mind."

"I hope I haven't done anything to displease you."

"Not at all. It's just problems at work, nothing for you to worry about."

He led me into the building by my leash and made our way to the elevator. On the way up I began to think about work. I wondered if anyone from the office even realized I was missing by then or did they still think I was off visiting some sick family member, as Devlin had told them.

Once inside Devlin put the bags down. "Get out of those clothes while I go get the rest.

"Yes, Master."

I went to the bedroom but instead of stripping I sat down on the edge of the bed. It felt nice to wear clothes again and I wanted to prolong the feeling. I browsed through some of my new things and wondered about what it would be like at this club Devlin was taking me to.

"What's this? Still dressed?"

"I'm sorry Master. I was just … "

He cut me off before I could blurt out some lame excuse as to why I still had my clothes on.

"I told you to strip. Apparently I have to get the punishment book out."

"Yes Master. I'm sorry Master."

I rushed to remove my clothes while cursing myself for being so foolish. He had been so generous today buying me all of those new clothes and shoes and we aren't home even five minutes and I'm already upsetting him.

After I finished undressing, I sat on the bed not knowing what else to do. He came in, smiling this time.

"Much better."

"We have a bit before we need to head out to get your hair and makeup done. Do you want to take a nap before then?"

I reached up, grabbing Devlin by his hand and pulling him closer to me, positioning his body between my legs.

"I would. Will you join me?"

I didn't give him a chance to answer before pulling his body on top of mine and kissing him.

He rolled over, laying his head on the pillow and positioning my head on his chest. I loved lying with him like that. He started running his fingers through my hair and I was out like a light. It's funny how something as simple as shopping can take so much out of you.

Devlin woke me up about an hour later. And by woke me up of course I mean, he stuck his mouth on my breasts and began biting on my nipples.

On the way to get my hair and makeup done I finally had to ask more about tonight.

"What club are we going to Master?"

He grinned. "It's not a club, it's the club. It's a private, member's only club. It's been around in some form or another for hundreds of years. There are locations all around the world, Houston, Dallas, Paris, London, Berlin, New York, San Francisco, Barcelona, Bora Bora, Zurich, and even Budapest."

"So it's like a country club with lots of international locations?"

"Not exactly. Not just anyone can be a member. In Houston we have one hundred and forty three male members, seventeen females. It's not easy to gain membership."

"Each of the members pay annual dues and those funds cover the facility costs as well as a few events that we hold each year. The building is open all year but most members only show up for special parties."

"Can you go to any of the clubs, like say you are visiting Bora Bora, or do you have to be a member for each city?"

"Membership is universal. If you are a member of the Houston branch, your benefits include all the services and privileges for all cities and countries around the world."

On the surface this club sounded like some sort of fancy business club for the rich and powerful but knowing Devlin in the way that I do now, I suspect it's much more than that. It was far more likely that it was all just a cover for a private sex club with girls held in cages and strippers hanging from the ceiling.

Chapter 10

Before getting out of bed I realized that I desperately needed to use the restroom and asked permission.

"No, you may not."

"But Master I really have to pee," I pleaded.

"You will just have to hold it. You need to learn that I'm in complete control of you and your body. I will tell you when you may go."

I felt the pressure of my full bladder and hoped I could hold on until he gave me permission.

"For now we are going to sort out what you are wearing tonight."

He pulled out the black backless dress with the extremely low cut front and placed it on the bed. He looked through the new shoes that we purchased and picked out the pair he wanted me to wear with the dress. I really wanted to wear the black pumps with little black spikes coming out of them but he decided he would rather me wear the plain black platform pumps instead.

"Try it on. I want to make sure this is perfect for tonight."

Trying to ignore the overwhelming need to use the bathroom, I slipped dress on.

"Slip the shoes on too," he commanded.

I bent down to put on my shoes, placing more strain on my bladder.

"You look fantastic. Come and have a good look at yourself."

There was a big floor to ceiling mirror set into one of the walls in the entrance hall. I got down on my hands and knees and crawled after him.

"Stand up," he said and I scrambled off the floor, the urge to pee becoming almost overwhelming. I stood up and looked in the mirror. I had to admit that I looked good. The low cut of the dress was extremely sexy. It was skimpier than I would normally have worn but I liked how I looked in it.

The pressure on my bladder caused me to cross my legs and I felt the sharp sting of the crop.

"Uncross your legs."

"I'm sorry Master, I just really have to go potty. May I please go to the restroom?"

"No and don't ask me again. I will tell you when you may go."

I uncrossed my legs but the urge was becoming unbearable.

"Go and take your outfit off."

I crawled back into the bedroom and removed my clothes, setting them neatly on the bed. He came back into the bedroom and I kneeled in front of him. By now I could think of nothing but the urge to relieve my bladder. I put my hands between my legs in an attempt to relieve some of the pressure. He saw this and gave me a hard stroke of the crop across my thigh.

"Stop that," he said, clearly getting angry with me. But I couldn't help it, the urge was unbearable.

"Come into the bathroom."

I crawled after him. He turned around and ordered me to stand up. When I did the pain of the pressure on my bladder caused my eyes to tear up.

With a wicked grin on his face, he turned on the tap. I couldn't stand it. The sound of the running water and the pressure on my bladder was pure torture. The next thing I knew I felt a hot stream of urine dribbling down my leg. I tried to stop it but I was too far gone by now. The stream became a flow and before I could help it I was peeing on the marble floor of the bathroom. My face turned bright red as I nearly died from embarrassment.

He looked at me, as if he was amused and said "Well it looks like you were not able to pass that test. Don't worry, it takes time to learn complete control and I hope I have taught you that the toilet is a privilege, not a right."

"Yes Master," I whispered totally mortified.

"I'll go and get a mop and bucket and you will clean up in here and then have a shower after."

"Yes Master."

He returned shortly and the bucket was full of hot soapy water and smelled of disinfectant. I began to clean up my mess, trying my best to hold back the tears. I was mortified and humiliated.

"This incident will not be recorded in the punishment book since it wasn't a willful act of defiance."

"Thank you Master."

Grateful for that at least, I took the mop and finished cleaning the floor. When it was completely cleaned up I put the mop in the bucket and stood them in a corner.

"May I take my shower now?"

"Yes you may."

"Thank you Master."

I stepped into the shower and scrubbed my skin as if to scrub my shame away. I couldn't believe that I peed on myself in front of Devlin. It was easy to wash my body clean, but a lot harder to wash away the embarrassment. Knowing I would have to face him sooner or later, I reluctantly turned off the water and got out of the shower. I wrapped myself in the soft fluffy towel he set out for me and dried myself off.

I went back into the bedroom and I heard him call to me. I crawled into the kitchen and he told me to sit at the table. I could not look him in the face. I accepted the cup of coffee he held out to me and began to sip it.

"Look at me," he said and I reluctantly raised my eyes to meet his.

"What happened was an exercise in control. You did quite well and I'm pleased with you. So let's put this behind us and get on with our evening."

"Yes, Master."

He grabbed a plate off of the counter and put it in front of me, urging me to eat the dinner he had made for me.

"Are you looking forward to going out tonight?"

"I am Master, but I'm also a bit nervous."

"No need to be nervous, it's just a small gathering. Several Masters and their slaves. It is nothing formal, you aren't to be presented tonight."

I wondered what he meant but held my tongue. I figured I would find out soon enough. Still, I couldn't help but feel a bit excited about going out tonight. Who knew, there might be a means of escape although I did not hold out too much hope, especially if this place had several other men like Devlin with their own slaves.

After dinner we cleaned up and headed out. He took me to a nearby beauty salon where they fixed my hair and did my makeup. I didn't normally wear a lot but the way they applied it with big smoky eyes, I felt really sexy. They painted my fingernails and toenails a bright red that also perfectly matched my lipstick. I was so made up, I could hardly recognize myself.

"You look perfect," he said while smiling at me.

"Thank you, Master."

Devlin was wearing a black custom tailored three piece suit and for a moment I thought how handsome he looked. I quickly pushed such ideas out of my head reminding myself that no matter how good looking he was, this man was holding me against my will.

On the way to the club he told me there were a few rules he wanted to go over.

"Firstly you are to address the Masters and Mistresses as "Sir" or "Ma'am" at all times. How you act reflects on me, so I expect you to be on your best behavior."

"Yes, Master."

"Under no circumstances are you to get drunk. I will leave it to your discretion as to how much you drink but any drunken behavior will go in the punishment book."

I was never really a big drinker, so I didn't think that would be an issue.

"If anyone asks who you belong to you are to answer that you are the property of Master D."

"Yes, Master."

"I think that just about covers it all do you have any questions?"

"Will I be on the leash all night or will I be free to roam about the party?"

"If you're a good girl, I may let you mingle with the others."

"Thank you, Master."

When we arrived I expected to see a bouncer with a clipboard standing at the club's big double doors to let people in. But that wasn't the case at all. We pulled up to a building that was reminisce of those old Atlanta plantations with big Grecian columns. We entered the front door by using a keycard, which brought us into a small room with a table towards the back. On top of the table was a large black box. Devlin opened the box and placed his hand in it and after a few beeps and the scan of his palm, a door to the left unlocked. It was all very cloak and dagger.

We walked through the doors and entered a low-lit room that had a 1980s lounge vibe. There were a handful of small tables, and a raised stage. Devlin said that sometimes they have live music.

We continued walking through and turned a corner, with another large locked door. Devlin used his keycard to gain entry.

When we stepped in, it was like we went through a portal in time. The entire place felt so 1920s Hollywood, very glamorous and elegant. The room was massive and had huge vaulted ceilings. The room was dripping with luxury. There were elaborate statues everywhere and several huge crystal chandeliers hanging from the ceiling.

I couldn't help but wonder if that is how little orphan Annie felt the first time she walked into Daddy Warbuck's mansion.

Off in the distance I could see about a dozen people, dressed mostly in leather, rubber or black denim. Many were holding a leash with a slave attached to the other end by means of collars like mine.

We walked down a red carpet to enter the room that was lined with about ten people standing on each side, wearing black hooded monk cloaks. When we walked past them, they didn't speak or even look up at us.

I wanted to ask Devlin who the people were but was too nervous. Instead I just continued walking behind him quietly, taking in my surroundings.

There was quite a mixture of people. There were women with male slaves, males with female slaves and the odd woman with a female slave. There did not appear to be any men with male slaves though and I asked Devlin about this.

"You will meet gay people at bigger gatherings, but the regular crowd is for the most part, straight."

A tall older gentleman came over and warmly greeted Devlin.

"I see you have a new girl, very nice."

"Yes she is," said Devlin. "Although not fully trained yet, but she has great potential."

"Would you care for a drink? There is champagne on the table over there," the man asked Devlin. "Your slave might like one too."

Very glad of the offer I said "Thank you Sir" as he led us over to the table.

"Good manners," the man said to Devlin, in obvious approval.

We got our drinks and I sipped mine hoping it would make me less nervous. I remembered his admonition about getting drunk though and vowed to go easy on the drinks.

There was music playing in the background and the whole atmosphere appeared sophisticated and well behaved. I was beginning to wonder what I had been worried about.

However, with all the security, it looked like there would be little opportunity to escape. I began to relax and looked around the room. Not all of the slaves were on leashes, some were just sitting on their Master's lap and others at their Master's feet. Curious, I asked Devlin about it.

"Well, they don't need to be. In fact all the slaves in this room don't need to be leashed. Some like it though when going out. It makes them feel secure."

"You mean all the slaves are here of their own free will Master?"

"Yes, they love their Masters and love being owned by them."

This came as a surprise to me. I hoped asking my next question wouldn't anger him.

"Then why, Master did you take me by force?"

"I have wanted you for a long time and I had to have you."

I was shocked by this revelation.

"You will grow to love me in time," he told me earnestly.

I remained quiet, sipping my champagne trying to take in what he had told me. He loved me that I wasn't expecting. He must have been planning this for months, or maybe even longer. This was no spur of the moment thing and I was in deeper than I had at first realized. However the wasn't the place to contemplate this, so I put it out of my mind for the time being.

People drifted over to us and I was introduced to them as they came. The men for the most part looked me up and down and said "nice", as if giving me their approval of my looks somehow mattered.

One or two asked when the initiation was going to be and Devlin told them, "A bit later on," without revealing what this initiation was about. I wanted to know though. Clearly it's important or so many people wouldn't keep bringing it up.

"When we were on our own, I asked. "What initiation, Master?"

"Oh just a custom the club has. All the new slaves go through it, but it's nothing for you to worry about for now. Just relax and enjoy yourself."

A beautiful blonde lady approached us with a sly grin on her face. She wasn't tall on her own, but she wore extremely high platform boots that added to her height.

"Hello Miss Rey. It's nice to see you again."

"I think you mean Mistress Sophie."

"Yes, of course Mistress Sophie," Devlin replied with a tinge of belligerence in his voice.

She looked me up and down with keen interest.

"Well, well. What do we have here?" She put her black gloved hand under my chin, forcing me to look up at her.

"I didn't realize you liked them so young Master D."

"She's of age," Devlin replied, not seeming too interested in engaging her in further conversation.

"How old are you my child?"

"I'm almost twenty-two ma'am."

"Interesting. I wouldn't have pegged you to be a day over fifteen."

She walked around me, as if she was inspecting merchandise. She gently rubbed her hand on my ass and then stroked my arm. She had such a gentle touch, it was hard to imagine her as a Dom.

"Such a pretty little thing, isn't she?" Then she just walked away.

I felt in need of another drink and asked if I might have one. "Of course," he said and we went over to the bar. I thought about asking him to take off the leash but I felt safer wearing it. The people here made me nervous.

A murmur went up through the crowd and I could feel the excitement in the air. Wondering what was going on, I asked Devlin about it.

"It seems that one of the slaves has been naughty all day and her Master has had enough. He's going to punish her."

I was shocked "You mean in front of all these people, Master?"

"Yes," he grinned. "Should make a good show." He headed over towards another corner room, followed by the people around us.

We found there was quite a crowd when we got there and it looked like we might not be able to see. I was relieved, I didn't really want to watch. Then someone said, "Let the new girl get a look" and we were propelled to the front of the crowd.

A man dressed in black leather was sitting on a sofa with a girl over his knee. She wore a leather corset and a leather thong panties, which he pulled down to reveal her ass.

"She has been sassy all day," the man said to the crowd.

There were murmurs of assent as he brought his hand down hard on her left cheek. When he lifted his hand I could see a hand print across her ass. He did the same on her right cheek and she was left with a scarlet hand print on each cheek. The crowd applauded and he began to spank her in earnest. Her ass turned from white to pink to bright red as he continued spanking her. He carried on, obviously enjoying entertaining the crowd.

Finally he stopped punishing her. Standing up, he threw the girl over his shoulder, like a caveman, and carried her up the stylish marble staircase, which Devlin said there were several bedrooms. I was ashamed to admit it but watching him spank her had turned me on.

Devlin saw the expression on my face and laughed.

"That aroused you didn't it my sweet?"

I denied it but he knew I was lying. Flushed, I sipped my drink and tried to look away.

A friend of his came over and took Devlin to one side to speak to him in private. I could make out some of what they were saying. There was some mention made of my initiation then he asked Devlin something else I couldn't hear. "Not tonight, she's not ready." Devlin told the man.

The way everyone keeps bringing up this initiation, I really couldn't help but be curious about it. I know Devlin said it's not something I should worry about for now, but obviously it's important or so many people wouldn't keep bringing it up.

"Master, do you mind if I get some food? I'm feeling a little peckish."

"Of course, my sweet," he said as he unclipped me.

I felt a little nervous about being in this place with Devlin and was reluctant to leave his side.

"Go on then, I'll be here when you are finished."

"Thank you Master."

I walked to the buffet table and got myself a plate of various cheeses and finger foods. A man standing next to me looked at me and smiled. He put his hand on my ass and asked me who owned me. I jumped back, trying to get out of his reach.

"I'm the property of Master D."

He put his hand inside of my dress and pinched my nipple. It hardened immediately and he laughed. He pulled my dress aside, to reveal my entire breasts and then leaned down and sucked on my nipple. I flushed bright red, embarrassed that this man I don't even know was touching me in such an intimate way.

"Very nice," he said. I pulled my dress back over and covered my exposed breast. "I will ask your Master if I may use you tonight."

I was horrified at the thought and could only hope Devlin would say no. Suddenly not hungry any more, I put down my plate of food and made my way back to Devlin.

When he saw me, he laughed. "Been making new friends?"

I said nothing and stayed by his side from then on only venturing away to get another drink. I hadn't forgotten his warning about getting drunk, but I was far from intoxicated. The alcohol just helped me to relax a little and I had a feeling I was going to need it before the night was out.

By now several people had come over and asked when the initiation was going to be. "Soon," he replied each time. I began to grow more apprehensive.

After a while, Devlin turned to me and said, "It's time for your initiation."

I felt butterflies fill my stomach. We went over to where the girl had received her punishment and Devlin called for everyone to gather round. "It is time for her initiation," he said. There were whistles and claps from the dominants as they formed a circle around us.

"Strip," Devlin commanded.

"Oh no," I said and started to back away.

He grabbed me by the arm firmly and whispered in my ear. "That goes into the punishment book, now behave yourself."

Knowing I had no choice, I pulled the dress over my head. I heard a lot of whistles and nearly froze. Only the thought of the punishment book enabled me to take my thong off. I stood in the middle of a group of strangers stark naked and utterly horrified.

"Let her initiation begin," Devlin proclaimed.

An orderly queue formed made up of all those who wished to take part.

"First we have the inspection," Devlin told the crowd.

The first man stood in front of me and looked me up and down, running his hands over my body and cupping my breasts. He ran his hand over my ass and said to Devlin, "Nice markings."

He parted my labia and ran his hand over my pussy. "Nice," he said and made way for the next man.

This man sucked on my nipples and inserted two fingers in me. He told me to bend over and I obeyed, afraid to do anything else. He ran his hands over my ass and stuck a finger up my asshole. He wasn't remotely gentle about it either.

The next person was a woman. She was very pretty and ran her hands over my breasts. Her touch felt different to the men's. I felt her soft lips on my nipples and felt her stroke my pussy until it opened. She then applied just the right amount of pressure on my clit so that it actually felt good. She kissed me on the mouth and reluctantly left me for the next man in line. This went on for almost an hour. So many men, feeling me, prodding me, sucking, and licking.

Despite my disgust with many of the people touching me, I did feel a little stimulated. I couldn't help it, my body just seems too react to being touched, even if I don't want it to. He made me feel dirty and ashamed.

Another woman sucked on my nipples then applied pressure on my clit until I nearly came. She kissed me passionately on the lips then stuck a finger up my asshole. I was aroused beyond belief. At last, everyone who wanted a turn to inspect me had finished. Devlin appeared by my side and whispered into my ear "You are doing well."

I breathed a sigh of relief thinking that it was at last over but he had another announcement to make to the crowd.

"Okay my friends, time for the spankings." Leading me over to the sofa, he bent me over the arm and grinned at the crowd. "One at a time please."

I was horrified. I was to be spanked by anyone who wanted a turn. The first man used his hand and spanked me long and hard. The next man removed his belt and gave me six strokes with it. The next spanked me with a slipper. One woman used her crop and laid three strokes across my ass. Another man ran his hand over my ass gently before spanking me hard.

It was horrible and painful and I couldn't help but sob uncontrollably as I was spanked by practically every person in the room. My rear was on fire. I thought the ordeal was over when someone said "Now last but not least, a spanking from her Master."

A cheer went up from round the room and I felt myself lifted off the arm of the chair and draped across Devlin's lap. There were murmurs and cheers of approval coming from the crowd I felt his hand come down hard on my ass. He smoothed away the pain with the flat of his hand before smacking me hard again. He began to rain smacks down on my ass hard and heavy. It seemed to go on forever when finally he stopped. He put his hand between my legs and felt my arousal.

"Well, wet already. That's my girl." He smacked me hard once more.

He let me go and I sat up. My face was as red as my ass. Someone tossed me my clothes. I caught them but before I could put them on Devlin lifted me up into his arms and carried me off to one of the bedrooms upstairs.

He kicked the door closed behind him and laid me on the bed. I was still clutching my clothes and he took them out of my hand and put them to one side. I felt his mouth on my nipple, sucking and licking. He took the other nipple into his mouth and flicked his tongue over it. He traced a path down my body with his tongue until he came to my pussy. Spreading it wide with his hands, he flicked his tongue over my clit.

My pussy began to twitch in response. He explored my hole, thrusting his tongue deep inside me. He moved up my body until I could feel his hard cock at my opening, before pushing past my entrance. At first he fucked me with easy strokes. His kisses were playful, interspersed with tiny bites.

Physically and mentally what I had just gone through with the initiation was painful, but somehow being here with Devlin like this, made all of that just go away. What kind of crazy voodoo was this man practicing on me?

It was more than just the sex -- but the sex was amazing. It was intense, but also tender at the same time. As he thrust inside of me I could feel the weight of the world lifting away and my body melt into his.

I saw the door had opened and someone was watching us. There was a man outlined in the doorway, his slave on her knees sucking him off. I was too far gone with lust to be able to stop. I just carried on fucking Devlin while this stranger watched and thrust his cock into his slave's mouth.

Hungry for more, I pushed my hips upwards matching his thrusts. He began diving into me with more urgency and I started to feel the tingling and knew I was about to come as well. He rammed his cock hard inside of me, all the way to the hilt. My entire body was alive and screaming for release.

By now I did not care about the man in the doorway although I could see him if I turned my head to the side. I cried out in pleasure as Devlin continued to thrust into me. I could feel myself losing control.

He pushed his body against me one last time, spilling his seed inside of me. It was just enough to push me over the edge and finally I exploded with pleasure as well. Our bodies dissolved together and shook, clutching at each other, while low grunts and soft moans escaped our mouths.

I felt a sudden pang of affection for him that I couldn't explain. What happened to me earlier, with the initiation, should have made me infuriated, but after my intimate time with Devlin I had this softness in my heart, even if tomorrow my body would be aching.

I heard a grunt from the visitor in the doorway as he came. I was still too deep in my own pleasure to say anything and when I next looked he had gone. I told Devlin of our visitor and he laughed, explaining that some people like to watch. He didn't seem too concerned so I tried to put it out of my mind.

We got dressed and went back out to the party. As we did I began to wonder how much longer we would have to stay because I was getting tired. Devlin though didn't seem ready to go, so I put on my best smile and stood by his side as we rejoined the others.

Chapter 11

Devlin turned to me. "Go and mingle now, it's time you met some of the people while you are wearing clothes."

I felt myself flush, thinking back on my initiation where I was buck ass naked. I wasn't keen to leave his side, but he gave me a push and said "Go on," so I wandered off on my own.

A drink seemed a good idea so I went to the bar to get one. A man handed me a glass of champagne.

"Thank you, Sir."

"Such a polite girl. A credit to your Master." He looked me up and down and nodded. "Yes, you would be a credit to any man."

Someone else joined us and I said "Hello Sir," when introduced. By now I had consumed a few drinks and, while not drunk, was beginning to feel a bit lightheaded.

"Come sit down with us," one of the men said and I let them lead me away from the drinks table. I barely noticed when we went through an archway and into one of the Arabian themed nooks in the room.

It was part of the main room but thanks to all of the decorations including several large plants, the view was somewhat skewed. The lighting was dim and the oversized sofa was surrounded by sheer drapes, giving those inside even more privacy. I sat on the sofa like bed and sipped my drink.

We were joined shortly by another man who sat next to me. I was tired and my mind was a bit clouded by the alcohol, so it didn't hit me right away that I was hidden in a corner with three strange men. The man sitting next to me put his arm around me and kissed me. I made a feeble protest but he paid no attention.

I heard some whispering amongst the men, then I felt the top of my dress being pushed aside to reveal my nipples. I felt strange mouths on my breasts sucking and licking at them. Before I knew what was happening, there was one man at my head, holding my hands down while another was at my feet, securing me in place.

It all happened so fast I didn't have time to react. I felt strongly out of it, as if I wasn't in control of my senses. The third man rubbed his hand up and down my thigh and then ran his hand between my legs, over my panties.

"Responsive girl, I like them like that."

I wasn't turned on by these men touching me. If they were feeling any wetness in my panties it was from Devlin's seed from earlier. Still, I couldn't think of a way to make these men stop touching me. I felt somehow removed from the situation.

"Turn her over," one of the men ordered and I was flipped over onto my stomach and my dress was pushed up, exposing my ass. Luckily I still had my panties on, perhaps not for long though.

Suddenly I felt the slash of a crop across my ass. It was followed by another slash and then I heard Devlin's voice. I felt so relieved. I tried to sit up but Devlin put his foot down and held me in place.

"What do you think you are doing?"

"We were just having a bit of fun," said one of the men.

"Yes, we no harm meant," said another.

"Did you have my permission?"

"Well, no but we didn't think you would mind."

"Just make sure you have permission next time," Devlin responded in an angry tone.

There were general mumblings of "sorry" from the men and they left.

The crop slashed down across my ass.

"What do you think you were doing?" I didn't know what to say. The crop hit me twice more. "You seemed to be enjoying yourself."

I felt the sting of the crop across my thighs.

"I was lured in here Master," I tried to explain. "I was a bit light headed and didn't notice where I was at first. I only realized there were three men in here with me when it was too late.

"Master," I pleaded "I was a bit light headed from the alcohol. I'm sorry."

I felt the sharp sting of the crop across my ass again.

"I warned you about getting drunk."

"I was not drunk Master, just a little light headed." I cried out as he hit me once again across the thighs.

"No one touches you without my consent, is that clear?"

"Yes, Master. I'm sorry."

"You will be sorry, very sorry. This definitely goes in the punishment book." I felt several more strokes of the crop against my ass. "Straighten your clothes we are leaving."

I quickly fixed my clothes, covering up my exposed breasts and followed obediently behind Devlin. No one else seemed to have noticed what happened and I was grateful there were no staring eyes. He went around the room and said his goodbyes before clipping my leash back on and leading me to the car.

On the way home he didn't say a single word to me. I knew he was angry and that scared me. I knew that he was going to punish me tonight, and it was going to be severe.

Once we were in the living room he ordered me to remove my clothes and to wait for him in the bedroom.

"I will come for you when I calm down."

It took about half an hour before he finally called for me to come to him. I got on my hands and knees and reluctantly crawled out to him. He was in the kitchen, sipping a cup of coffee and had my punishment book open in front of him.

"I understand how the incident happened and I accept that you were not entirely responsible for what went on. However, you still must be punished severely for your conduct. You need to learn to listen to what I tell you."

"Yes, Master."

"Before we start I want you to understand why you are being punished. You are my property and no one else's. Sometime in the future I may allow another Master to use you but only with my express permission."

He looked at me and I saw the hurt in his eyes.

"Had such permission been given tonight?"

"No, Master."

"Those men should not have taken you off. However, more to the point you should not have gone with them. Had you been sober you would not have gone would you?"

"No Master, I wouldn't have gone." It was then I realized he was jealous and my heart fluttered.

"Alright, this is what I have decided. For refusing to take your clothes off at the initiation, three strokes of the cane. For your disgraceful behavior with those men it will be thirty strokes of the cane, five of which will be across the pussy."

I knew I couldn't take that many. I was still sore from the beating I had taken from my initiations. It was then it dawned on me that he had said five were to be across the pussy. I gasped in horror.

"Believe me you are getting off lightly."

I shivered in apprehension. I didn't know how I was going to make it through this. I felt like I was about to be sick.

"I want you to lie on top of the table first."

I climbed up, trembling, and laid down on the wooden surface while he put my ankles in the cuffs. Next he fitted my wrists into the cuffs above my head.

"I will exempt you from having to thank me after each stroke. I doubt you will be in any condition to speak."

I felt him tap the cane lightly against my mound, carefully measuring the distance. There was a swish and then a searing, white-hot pain that shot through my body.

"One. Four more to go."

The next lash of the cane hit me with full force across my defenseless pussy. I let out a loud wail and he struck me three more times, leaving angry purple marks. I screamed out in pain, begging for mercy, with tears rolling down my face. I struggled to get away without any luck.

"That is all for the front."

My pussy throbbed with an agonizing pain.

"Please no more," I begged him but he didn't listen. Instead he just unfastened my restraints and repositioned my body. I didn't know how I was going to get through the rest of my punishment. Perhaps I would get lucky and pass out.

The same thought must have occurred to Devlin because he left me laying there and returned with a bowl of water and a sponge.

"Cold water to keep you alert."

He helped me off the table then bent me over its smooth wooden surface. He attached my wrists to the restraints leaving me with my ass exposed for further punishment. I still had twenty eight more strokes to look forward to.

He took up his position behind me and I felt the first stroke burn like fire across my ass. It was followed by another in the same spot. He was deliberately laying the strokes on slowly to give the pain time to sink in.

Another deliberate blow struck me across the thighs. Another blow fell and then another. I heard myself cry out, a strangled, almost animal-like cry of pain. But it fell on deaf ears. Devlin just continued hitting me with the cane over and over again.

He stopped for a minute to wipe my face down with cold water. Then the strokes resumed again. Hard stinging blows. Deliberately placed to cause as much pain as possible. He stopped again and sponged down my face. He resumed the punishment and I felt a stroke along the crack of my ass. There were many more strokes and I began to grow faint.

I heard his voice as if it were far away.

"That is fourteen."

Things began to turn grey and I passed out. I came to with him sponging my face down with ice cold water.

"Looks like you passed out there."

The burning of my ass and throbbing of my pussy soon reminded me where I was. I groaned, realizing my nightmare wasn't over yet.

"Your punishment is now half over."

"Please Master, no more," I begged.

"When I pass sentence, I will always carry it out, no exceptions. And as I told you before, once the punishment has been carried out, there will be no more mention of the offense. You will start again with a clean slate."

That's all well and good, I thought, but I still had fourteen more strokes of the cane to endure. He put down the sponge and resumed his position. Despite being restrained, my body shook. I felt the burning pain of the next stroke across my thighs. There was a long pause then the next stroke hit me across the ass. Another long pause and he laid another stroke across my left cheek. My body was trembling uncontrollably.

Gently increasing his tempo, several more strokes landed on the same spot as previous strokes. I didn't think I could stand much more, especially as the cane bit deep into my tortured flesh. Swish, swish, swish, swish.

I thought I surely would pass out again, but I didn't. I was totally conscious for the rest of the strokes.

"There, your punishment is over."

He undid the restraints but I just laid there, unable to move. He gathered me into his arms and carried me to the bedroom. He laid me down, bent over and kissed me.

I winced as my ass made contact with the bed. He noticed this and gently rolled me over onto my stomach and covered me with the sheet.

"You had better sleep on your front tonight."

I heard his footsteps retreating from the bedroom and cried into my pillow. I didn't know how I was going to get any sleep. My pussy and ass were both on fire. Even the light touch of the sheet hurt.

Chapter 12

I laid in the dark for a long time, the pain keeping me awake. Eventually, as the birds began to sing, I drifted off. I must have slept most of the day because when I woke the sun was low in the sky.

I was very stiff and found it hard to move. I managed to turn over and sit up in bed. He must have heard me because he appeared at the bedroom door.

"Do you need any help sitting up?"

"Yes, please."

I was grateful for the offer. He came over to the bed and arranged my pillows and helped me sit up properly.

"I thought you might like something to eat. I'll help you to the bathroom and then come back with your food."

After using the restroom I stood up and looked at myself in the mirrors. Seeing the welts across my body made the memories all come flooding back. As I started to cry, he poked his head in the bathroom.

"Are you ok?"

"Yes, I'm sorry. I'm just coming out."

He helped me back to the bed and arranged the pillows so I could sit up more comfortably.

He sat down next to me and fed me an assortment of fresh fruits and cheeses. In the middle of the tray was a delicious dip. There were grapes, strawberries, raspberries, blueberries, little cubes of watermelon and cantaloupe. He also had three kinds of cheese, Cheddar, Gouda and Swiss, cut up into little bite sized squares.

"I love this dip. What's in it?"

He gave me a big smile. "I'm glad you like it. It's my favorite. It's a mixture of cream cheese and marshmallow crème with just a dab of cool whip."

"I just love it. It's so sweet. Did it come with the fruit tray or was it part of a mix?"

"I made all of this myself. It's not a pre-bought fruit platter from the store."

"Seriously? You made all of this? How?"

"It's not that complicated. I just bought the type of fruits and cheese I thought you might like, cut them up into small pieces and arranged them on the tray. The fruit dip is something that I've been making for years. It's a family recipe."

"I can't believe it. You never cease to amaze me Master."

I really had to admit, I never thought Devlin would be the kind of guy that would also have any sort of domestic skills. Sure he had been making me food while I was here but it was mostly simple things like toast and eggs and pasta. This fruit platter was so fancy with so much attention to detail. And the dip, oh that dip, so beyond delicious.

After breakfast he ran a bath for me and I soaked in a warm tub with bath salts that helped sooth my aching muscles and sensitive skin. We spent the rest of the day watching old movies and just enjoying each other's company.

We talked about his love of cooking and I found out he even knows how to make his own Mozzarella. He promised to make some for me soon. Although my body still ached from the beating of the night before, the day was still wonderful. It was intimate and genuine without being sexual and for the first time in a long time, I spent the entire day happy.

I fell asleep that night on his lap watching a movie. He carried me to bed and when he covered me with a blanket and left the room, I felt a longing for him to stay with me. I hated that he didn't sleep in the same bed as me. I wanted to wake up the next morning wrapped in his arms.

As he started to pull away I grabbed his hand and gently tugged, letting him know that I wanted him to stay.

"It's late my slave, you need your rest. I'll see you in the morning."

He kissed my forehead and left my room. I didn't get what I wanted, but it was still a wonderful day I had with him and that is what I was thinking of when I drifted off to sweet slumber.

The next morning I awoke to Devlin entering my room with a breakfast tray. I sat up on my own, gleefully awaiting to see what he had made for me today. He sat down next to me and started feeding me bacon wrapped chicken bites and deviled eggs. While not your typical breakfast food, it was still mouthwateringly delightful.

"I have to head into the office for a bit. Will you be okay on your own for a few hours? There is a case I've been working on that really needs my attention."

"Of course, Master. May I have a book to read while you're away?"

He kissed my forehead. "That's a good girl. And yes I'll bring you a few books before I head out. For now go shower while I get dressed."

By the time I got out of the shower and shaved, he finished getting himself ready for work. He came back into my bedroom before leaving and as promised brought me a selection of books he thought I might like to read. He attached my restraints and headed off for the day.

Time passed quickly while he was at work, thanks to the book I was reading. It was a romance novel, a story about a girl who fell in love with her boyfriend's best friend. She would never act on her feelings for this other man but when she found out her boyfriend betrayed her with another woman, she went running to the other man's arms and that's when things got heated. And that's also just about the time Devlin returned.

"Were you a good girl while I was gone?"

"Yes, Master I was."

"I brought you a gift."

I looked up at him, unable to contain my excitement. "What is it?"

He handed me a box and inside I found a breathtakingly beautiful opal bracelet.

"It's so pretty. I can't believe you got this for me."

"I always thought relationships were like opals," Devlin said as he put it on my wrist.

"What do you mean?"

"They both must be handled with care. They are beautiful when they are new. It seems as if nothing could go wrong. However just as extreme temperatures can crack the opal, extreme emotions can cause cracks in a relationship. Over time these cracks can cause the relationship or the opal to shatter."

"I've never heard that before. That's so lovely and so true."

I held my wrist to my heart, which now donned the bracelet. "I promise to always handle with care."

"My family has been in Opal mining for generations."

Most of our mines are in Australia, but we also have a rather large mine in northeastern Brazil. We also have a small mine in Nevada, about two hours northeast of Las Vegas. In fact, on the day I was born they found a giant two hundred carat fire opal.

"Is this from one of your family's mines?"

"Yes, the stones in your bracelet are from one of our Australian mines."

My heart felt it was going to burst with joy. Devlin never talks about his family. It's almost as if over the years he has gone out of his way to avoid the subject at any cost. And now here he has not only revealed something about his family but also shared with me part of their legacy with this gift.

We enjoyed a late lunch together and then he had me get dressed. He didn't say where we were going, but I didn't really care. I was just happy to be getting out of the house.

When he got to the car he realized he needed to stop and get gas so we headed to a nearby station.

"Are you going to tell me where we are going yet Master?"

"You'll see."

He unfastened my leash and handed me some money, telling me I could go inside and get a fountain drink.

"Thank you Master. Do you want anything?"

"No. But hurry up, don't doddle. I want to get to where we are going?"

I kissed his cheek and ran inside the gas station. I was standing at the drink station trying to decide if I wanted a Coke or Pepsi when I heard someone calling my name.

"Elizabeth, is that you?"

The voice didn't sound familiar so I turned around to see who it was. It was Corbin Tedlow from work. He was an intern I worked with at Ashworth and Kent.

"Oh my God, Elizabeth it is you! I can't believe it. Everyone has been so worried about you."

He pulled me in for a big hug and I looked around nervously to make sure Devlin was still outside, pumping gas.

"It's so wonderful to see you as well Corbin."

"Are you coming back to work soon?"

"Well, I'm not sure. Things are still up in the air right now."

"You better Elizabeth, because you are missing all of the good gossip."

"Oh really? Do tell!"

Corbin was always such a great little gossip. I couldn't wait to hear what he had for me this time.

"It's about everyone's favorite office slut-bag."

Of course it was about Brianna Bristow, I always hated her. That girl is always doing something or someone.

"Well, the rumor is she has been spending a lot of time blowing a senior associate, during office hours, under his desk."

"No way!"

"Yes!"

When he said senior associate, my mind immediately went to Devlin and my heart sank. He wouldn't do that, right? Surely it wasn't him.

"Which senior associate?"

Corbin shrugged. "That's the thing, nobody seems to know which senior associate she's blowing."

"There are only six of them, and one of them is a female, so it can't be that hard to figure out," I said, desperately hoping he knew something more about the identity and praying it wasn't Devlin.

"All I can say for sure is it's not Walter, he's been out of the country for the last six weeks."

"Come on Corbin, you have to know more than that."

I laughed and playfully patted Corbin's arm and when I did I heard Devlin clear his throat.

"I came to see what was taking so long."

He glared at Corbin and then looked back at me. Corbin took a step back, putting more space between us.

I took a step towards Devlin and hooked my arm into his. The tension between Devlin and Corbin was intense and I realized that Devlin was jealous. I don't know why I liked it so much that he was, but much to my shame, I did.

"Devlin you remember Corbin Tedlow from work?"

Devlin nodded. "Of course."

Devlin put his hand out to shake Corbin's.

"Corbin was just telling me some juicy office gossip about a senior associate being naughty with the office ho-bag."

Corbin chuckled. "Hello Mr. Kent. It's nice to see you, it's been awhile."

"Yes, I guess it has been."

"We better get going," Devlin said. "We have a lot to get done. Corbin, it was nice seeing you again."

"Yeah. Elizabeth call me sometime soon and fill me in on what's going on. We miss you so much at work."

"I will, I promise," I said to Corbin as I walked off with Devlin or more specifically was dragged off.

When we got in the car Devlin didn't say anything but I knew he was upset. Still, all I could do was smile. I liked his possessive side, it was endearing. I was smiling to myself as we drove down the road, headed to who knows what location.

"What's so amusing?"

"Nothing, I was just thinking."

"Take off your panties?"

"What?" I turned to him surprised at what he was telling me to do?

"I said, take off your panties."

I did as Devlin asked me to and removed my panties. After he exited the highway and turned off onto a side road, before pulling into the parking lot of a nearby shopping center. I got a little worried that he might ask me to get out and bend over the car in the parking lot and spank my bare ass in public.

He got out of the car and went to retrieve a bag out of the trunk. I sat there quietly and watched him as he returned and opened up a box and put batteries into a shiny silver thing that was about two inches long and about an inch wide. He took out a tube of lube, rubbing it in, covering the entire little silver thing with a thin layer.

"Do you know what this is?"

"No Master, I don't."

"It's called a power bullet."

He put his hand between my legs and inserted it into my pussy and then turned it on. It was tiny but it packed a powerful punch as it started to vibrate against my clit.

I put my hand on the dashboard to secure myself. I flung my head back and let out a soft moan.

"Exactly what I thought."

"Huh?" I could barely concentrate, as the little bullet stimulated my clit. It felt so good.

"Your body is very responsive. Your inexperience makes it hard for you to control your urges. So even if you were upset with me, I could still make you come."

"That's so not true," I panted. "I'm not always turned on when touched."

"You are going to learn control starting today. You may not come until I give you permission."

"Yes, Master," I barely was able to say.

He put his hand on the silver bullet inside of me, tapped it, turning the speed up. He then started the car up and began driving again, taking us to whatever our final destination may be.

I was so distracted on trying not to come that I didn't pay attention to where we were going. After about fifteen minutes, I could barely stand it. I was trying everything I could to focus on anything but my body.

I tried hard to control my orgasm. I desperately needed release, but I also wanted to prove Devlin wrong. I wasn't responsive to any and every touch. I could control my body.

"How we doing over there?" Devlin teased.

It took me a moment to answer. "I'm fine. I'm fine."

I really thought I was. But as he turned the corner onto some side street, he drove over a bump and I just lost it. I let the coiling heat that's been building in me go, and my orgasm was so intense, it was almost blinding. I collapsed against the door and tried to regain control of my body and my brain.

Devlin pulled into a driveway and parked the car. He removed the silver bullet from my pussy and gave me my panties to put back on.

He came over to my side to let me out, as he always did. When he opened my door, I stood up and he shut the door behind me. I was still half out of my mind from my orgasm.

As I leaned against the car for support, Devlin stood in front of me, gloating.

"You are mine and I want you to make that clear to anyone you may be with at any given time."

He leaned in and spoke against my lips.

"I may not be your first kiss or your first love, but I promise you'll remember me a lot longer."

He feathered kisses along my jawline and I flung my head back as he ran his tongue down my neck. It was so erotic and sexy. Damn it. He's turning me on again. Maybe he was right. Maybe I really can't control my body.

When I looked up I recognized a tree. It was the pecan tree that was outside the window of my apartment. Pushing Devlin back I turned around to see that he had taken me to my place.

I couldn't believe my eyes. Devlin had brought me home. Did that mean he was releasing me? Was he tired of me? Was he letting me go? Was the rumor about someone having sex with Brianna at work really about him? Has he grown bored of me and decided to be with her instead? She did have far more sexual experience than me.

I opened my mouth to ask him, but then closed it without saying a word. What was I going to do, ask him if he was bored of me already?

What is wrong with me? I should be happy that he's letting me go. Yet I'm not. I had really started to have feelings for him. It wasn't always perfect but still, I thought we had something special, that maybe we could have really had a real relationship. I'm so ridiculous.

I started to walk inside when he grabbed my arm to stop me.

"Are you okay?"

"I'm fine Devlin. Let's just get this over with."

"Excuse me?"

"Listen, I get it, we don't have to drag this out. You want someone who is a little more experienced. I'm sure you and Brianna will be wonderfully happy."

I tried to pull away from him but he wouldn't let me. Instead he pulled me into his arms. I squirmed, trying to get free of his embrace, but he wasn't letting me go.

Cupping my face, he looked into my eyes. "I don't know what you think Mary Elizabeth, but I love you. I don't want to be with Brianna or anyone else but you."

I tossed a glance over my shoulder. "Why are we here then?"

"I thought you might like to pick up some things before the movers come this weekend and put everything else in storage."

"What do you mean? I don't understand. Why would they move my stuff into storage and what about my lease?"

"Since you are living with me now, there is no reason to keep this apartment anymore so I called your landlord and paid off your lease. Why pay rent on a place you are never at? It just doesn't make sense."

He leaned in, kissing me softly, moving to trace my lips with his.

"So you aren't the one having relations with Brianna at the office?"

He chuckled. "Why would you think that?"

"I don't know. There are only six senior associates, one is a female and one has been out of the country, so that meant there was a one in four chance it was you. Then I started thinking maybe you would be into having some slut crawl on her knees and sucking your cock."

"I'm glad to see you think so highly of me."

I sighed. "It's not that. It's just that she's far more experienced than me and I thought maybe that's what you were looking for."

He pulled me in for another kiss. "It's not even in the realm of possibility that I would ever want Brianna over you. Now let's put this silliness to rest and go inside and get some of your things that you want to bring back to the penthouse with you."

I grabbed some old boxes I had in my storage closet and started filling them up with a few of the things that were near and dear to me like family photo albums, my makeup case and my iPad.

We went into my bedroom and I began going through some of my clothes. I grabbed some jeans and set them on the bed but Devlin immediately returned them to my closet.

"I told you, no jeans."

I sighed and continued looking for suitable clothing. After packing up my clothes and a few other personal belongings, I gave them to Devlin who put them in the car. I took one last look at my place and realized that I wasn't as sad about the move as I probably should have been.

When we got back to the penthouse I put my things away in my bedroom and then Devlin called for me. He was holding a bottle of champagne.

"Thought you might like a drink to celebrate making our living together official."

"Thank you, Master."

I sat down at the kitchen table and sipped my glass of champagne, while Devlin prepared us something to eat. He made us roasted tomato bruschetta, mini roast beef sandwiches and baked, stuffed avocados.

By the time we finished eating I had several glasses of champagne and I began to feel a little light headed. Devlin led me into the living room and sat next to me on the couch.

"How about we play a game?"

I wasn't sure what he meant, but I suspected it was something sexual in nature.

"Sure. What did you have in mind?"

When a big grin came across his adorable face, I knew I was right. I knew he had sex on the brain.

"How about truth or dare?"

"Okay, who goes first?"

He placed his hand on my knee. "I'll go first. Truth or dare?"

I knew Devlin had a vicious streak so I thought it was best I picked truth. Selecting dare was far too risky.

"Truth."

"How many men have you been with before me?"

I felt my face turn fifty shades of red. "Uh, I change my mind. I want dare."

"It doesn't work that way my sweet. You chose truth so answer the question."

I tried to get away but with his hand on my leg he kept me in place.

"This isn't fun anymore. I don't want to play."

"I don't understand why you won't answer me. Are you afraid I'll think it's too many and that will somehow change the way I feel about you? You are a hot twenty one year old, I get that you've had partners before me. I don't care what the answer is, I just want you to be honest with me."

I didn't want to reply. I was embarrassed, but not because I had been with too many men. Just the opposite.

"Answer me Mary Elizabeth or this goes into the punishment book."

I looked down, not wanting to face him as I spoke.

"I took some classes at the community college and there was this guy I kept running into. Prior to him I didn't have a lot of serious boyfriends. But I was tired of being a virgin. I just wanted to get it over with. After a few weeks I finally agreed to go to his place for dinner, knowing what he wanted to happen. It was horrible and only lasted a few minutes. He spent more time putting the condom on then he was actually inside of me."

Devlin put his hand under my chin and forced me to look up at him.

"Is that the only time you've had sex before me?"

I shook my head no. "I thought that maybe that first time was just a fluke, like maybe he was nervous or something since it was our first time together so the next week I went out with him again. Like before he spent a lot of time putting his condom on, playing with his balls a lot and then finally put his cock inside of me. I don't remember exactly how long it was, but it was brief, maybe a few strokes before he grunted and then came. He rolled off of me and then got up to watch TV, without saying a word to me. It was all so horrible. I began to think that maybe sex just wasn't what everyone kept saying it was. Then I met you."

I had no idea you were so inexperienced when we got together. I knew you were tight, but damn, that puts a whole new spin on things. No wonder you are so responsive. You don't have any experience at all."

"So do you want truth or dare?"

"Truth," he responded with confidence.

"What was your first sexual experience?"

"I was seventeen. It was a girl I had been dating for a few months. We had sex while her parents were out of town. We spent the whole weekend together and had sex several times before they returned."

"What happened to her? Are you still friends?"

"I haven't seen her in years. While I was in law school I heard she got married and now has a gaggle of kids."

"Was she the first person that you spanked?"

"Oh no, that's not how this game works. If you want to ask me more questions, you have to wait until your turn. For now you must decide, truth or dare?"

"Truth."

"I noticed that night at the club you got turned on by one of the Mistresses touching you. Is that your fantasy to be with another woman?"

I felt my face turn bright red.

"It is, isn't it?"

"No. I mean to be honest, I liked how she felt when she touched me. It was nice. Different than you. It was soft and gentle. But I still prefer men."

"There is something you aren't telling me."

I took another drink of my champagne and continued.

"My fantasy isn't to be with another woman, it's to watch you with another woman. I haven't had a lot of experience with sex before and I would love to see your cock pushing in and out of another girl's pussy. I would love to watch her lips work their way up and down your shaft. I want to lay her on the bed, spread her legs apart and just explore her clit. I want to watch you ramming your cock inside of her. Is that crazy?"

"Not at all. I think it's something we should definitely explore someday."

I was embarrassed that I revealed my secret fantasy to him and so wanted to change the subject before he started asking me more questions about it.

"Your turn. Truth or dare?"

Devlin raised an eyebrow and then grinned. I was sure he was about to say truth when he surprised me and instead said "dare". I couldn't believe it. I took another drink of my champagne and then sat the glass down on the coffee table. I took Devlin's glass and sat it down next to mine and then I sat on Devlin's lap.

"I dare you to make love to me."

He leaned in to kiss me but I pulled back. "No, let me be clear. I mean make love to me, no bondage or spankings or servitude. I want passion and kisses and tenderness."

Devlin didn't answer me with words. Instead he just grabbed my hair, pulling my head back and started licking my neck and then forcing my face back down to his for a deep, passionate kiss that made my entire body tingle.

He stood up and I wrapped my legs around his waist and he carried me to the bedroom. Only we didn't go to my bedroom, this time he took me to his. It was the first time we had ever went to his room.

Laying me gently down on his bed, he began to remove my clothes and then his own. I wrapped my legs around his hips and held onto him. I felt him deep inside of me and with every slow and steady stroke, he heated me from the inside out. I rolled over and positioned myself on his lap so I could control the speed.

"Tell me what I want to hear," I said through gritted teeth.

He groaned as he moved his hips against mine in a way that stroked the deepest parts of me.

"I love you Mary Elizabeth and I want to spend the rest of my life showing you just how much."

I don't know why, but it literally made my pussy twitch when I heard him say that to me. My legs shook with exertion as I bounced up and down on his lap. My screams became moans and finally he had enough of letting me control the pace and took over. Rolling me over and throwing himself on top of me in a wild moment of raw lust.

He groaned and plunged into me, sliding so deep that I cried out. I dug my nails into his back and gasped as he slammed into me even harder.

He growled against my ear. "Come for me baby."

In that moment my body gave him everything I had. Every muscle in my body stiffened and my inner core spasmed around him so tightly that I felt him explode inside of me.

He collapsed on me, panting. After a while he gently withdrew from me and I curled into his body and he held me protectively in his arms. As he ran his fingers through my hair, I started to drift off to sleep. I loved being in his arms and listening to his heartbeat. His breathing steadied and he stopped playing with my hair. I realized he must have fallen asleep.

I closed my eyes and whispered "I love you," before falling into a deep slumber myself.

Chapter 13

When I woke up the next morning I was happy to find that Devlin was still asleep by my side. It was such a wonderful feeling to wake up in his arms. I didn't want to move and risk waking him up. So instead I laid there thinking about my life with Devlin. On the one hand, he was kind, considerate, loving and caring. He took such good care of me. On the other hand he could be harsh, strict and intolerant. He was holding me prisoner, a captive. That wasn't right.

I began to wonder why I hadn't made more of an attempt to escape before. He took me out. Surely I could have called to someone for help? Why didn't I? When I ran into Corbin I could have told him what was going on and asked him to help me escape. Despite everything that has happened, I think I am in love with him.

Devlin began to stir and since he was awake I decided to go to the bathroom, shower and get ready for the day. The moment I stepped out of the bed and started walking he cleared his throat. I stopped to look at him.

"What do you think you are doing?"

"I thought I would go take a shower."

"I don't recall giving you permission to walk."

"You are right Master. I'm sorry."

I went to my knees and reluctantly crawled out of his room, and into my own. I don't know why I thought things would be different between us after making love the night before. But they weren't. He's still just as harsh and just as strict.

After using the restroom I began to run the water for a bath when Devlin came in with a large jar of something purple in his hands and he started pouring it into the water.

"What's that?" I inquired.

"It's bath and body oil. It's supposed to be good for your skin."

That was so sweet of him to think of something like that for me and I gratefully stepped into the tub and began to relax in the warm, scented water.

After helping me wash my hair, Devlin left me alone to soak in the tub. By the time I got out, I could smell bacon in the air and knew he had breakfast ready. I dried off and crawled into the kitchen.

He gave me permission to sit at the table and together we enjoyed a wonderful breakfast. He didn't speak much, mostly he just read his paper but I could tell something was on his mind.

"Is something wrong Master? Are you upset with me about something?"

"Not at all my sweet. I was just thinking about last night."

"Please don't." I interrupted and he gave me a quizzical look. "Last night was the absolute best sexual experience of my life. Please don't ruin it by saying something negative or hurtful about it."

He chuckled and then motioned for me to come sit on his lap. When I did he put his arms around me and held me tight.

"I don't know why you think I wouldn't feel exactly the same way as you do about what took place last night. You know how wonderful it was to fall asleep with you secure in my arms?"

"Then what is weighing so heavy on your mind? You've been so quiet all through breakfast."

I put my forehead to his and we sat there quietly for a moment.

"As great as last night was, it's not who I am. I can never be that guy for you."

I leaned in for a deep, passionate kiss.

"I know, I really do. And that's part of what made last night so special, because it was different."

He smiled and patted my leg.

"I have to go out to meet with a client soon. Will you be okay here by yourself for a few hours?"

"Yes, Master."

I was disappointed that he was leaving me for so long but I also understood.

"I've also decided that I won't be locking you in today. I've given it a lot of thought and I realize the only way our relationship can move forward is to allow you to decide on your own if you want us to have a future together."

"Thank you, Master." I leaned in to kiss him before getting off of his lap and returning to my own chair.

He went to get ready for work while I cleaned up our breakfast dishes. When he left, he did as he promised and let me remain free of my restraints. I poured myself a cup of coffee and sipped it as I considered the implications.

To stay would be to opt for a life of slavery. I loved him but was I prepared for that deep of a commitment? What about my outside life? Would he allow me to communicate with my friends or family? I had not thought of it before, but life outside this penthouse was still carrying on. My job was still there waiting for me to return. My old life was there too. Admittedly, at times I had been lonely but was I prepared to give up my independent lifestyle altogether?

Could I give up all my rights to privacy for the rest of my life? Because to stay with Devlin, that is exactly what it would mean.

Even as I weighed up the difficult decision that faced me, I was smiling. I was in love there was no doubt about that. I couldn't explain it, but the heart wants what the heart wants, logic be damned.

Still, would it be enough to see us through? Was I ready to give myself to someone so completely? The one thing I knew for sure is that I would have to be very strong to go through life with him.

The unlocked door kept jumping into my mind. Perhaps it was a trick and it was really locked. Did I want to try it and find out? No, he definitely had not locked it when he went out. Did I stay here with the man I loved and give up my old life, or did I walk out the door leaving him behind but gaining my freedom?

Thoughts of that unlocked door flashed into my mind. What would it be like just to walk out the door? I squashed such thoughts and finished doing my hair. But the thoughts kept creeping back in. I could go downstairs and call a taxi and be back at my little place before an hour had passed. I could be free. Then I thought of his laugh, the way his eyes crinkled when he smiled, and I knew I loved him. I did not want my freedom, I wanted him.

Should I stay? Should I go? Should I stay? Should I go? It's all I could think about. I didn't know what to do and I had nobody to reach out to and talk about it. I felt so alone and trapped. My heart started racing and a fog of panic descended on me. I must be crazy not to want to get out of there. No one in their right mind would stay, would they?

I rushed to my bedroom and threw on some clothes. I remembered seeing my purse hidden at the very top of the closet. I fumbled around until I got my hands on it. Looking inside I found my keys were gone, but I knew he had them already. What mattered most is my wallet. It was still there with all of my money and credit cards inside. I could get a cab and go to a hotel somewhere until I figured out what I was going to do.

My heart pounding, I approached the door. I turned the knob slowly and opened it just a crack. I half expected him to be standing there by the elevator, but to my relief he wasn't there. I pushed the door open further. The foyer was deserted like always and I tentatively put a food over the threshold. One more step and I was out of his penthouse and to the elevator -- A mere seconds from freedom.

I closed the door behind me. Shaking with fear, I went over to the elevator and pressed the button. I heard it creaking its way up the floors and when it reached my floor, the doors slid open. I went to enter the elevator but suddenly I was paralyzed and couldn't make myself move a single muscle in my body.

The fog of fear had cleared. What the hell was I doing? I realized at that moment that I couldn't leave Devlin. Our relationship may not be perfect, but I loved him. I don't know how or why but I do, I really and truly loved him.

I rushed back to the ornate door. My hands were shaking so much that I had trouble opening it. I was terrified that he would come back and fine me in the foyer, near the elevator. Finally I got the door opened and was back inside the safety of the penthouse and nobody was the wiser.

I went to my bedroom to make sure that I put my purse back where it was hidden at the top of my closet and then took my clothes off before he came home. My collar was still intact because it was locked into place.

I fell onto my bed to take a nap, only when I did I heard a noise. Rolling over I found it, a folded up piece of paper. Inside was a handwritten note from Devlin that read, "Faith isn't something you find. It's something you have. Do you have faith in us?"

I don't know what made me panic like that earlier. And this letter, how sweet was that? I felt horrible about having second thoughts of our relationship and I vowed to never tell Devlin how close I came to running away.

I heard the bells and tell-tale clang of the elevator and knew that meant Devlin was home. I rushed to kneel by the door, how I knew he probably would like me to greet him when he got home.

The door opened and he stood there, his face breaking into a smile when he saw me. It was such a spontaneous smile and his eyes shone with genuine happiness. I was sure then that I had done the right thing in staying. However, as quickly as it had come, the smile was gone from his face and he looked angry.

"Follow me," he said and started off towards my bedroom. I wondered what I had done to change the smile to such anger in so short a time. I did not have to wait too long to find out.

"Sit down," he said as he patted a space on the bed beside him. When I was sitting next to him, he reached out and turned my face to meet his. I tried to avoid his gaze but he ordered "Look at me" and I did as he said.

"So, do you want to tell me why you left the penthouse this morning?"

I was about to deny it, thinking he couldn't possibly know about my panic earlier but before I could speak he interrupted.

"Don't make it worse by telling lies, I know all about it."

I didn't know what to say. How could he possibly know that I had left this morning?

"You might as well tell me the truth, because I will only punish you more if you lie."

"How did you know, Master?"

"I placed a piece of tape over the door and when you pushed it open, it broke it off. Simple really, but surprisingly effective. Luckily you changed your mind. Had you actually left I would have hunted you down and brought you back. Your punishment would have been a lot worse if I had to scour the city for you, believe me."

I did believe him too. I don't think he'll ever really let me go.

"Can you imagine how I felt when I came home and saw that the tape had been disturbed? Thinking I would open the door to find you gone and then finding you here after all. Do you realize what you put me through?"

"No Master, I didn't."

"I am too angry to talk any more right now."

He collected the wrist cuffs and a length of rope off the dresser and said "Come". He took me to where the big hook in the ceiling was and attached the wrist cuffs. He then took the piece of rope and threaded it through the cuffs and over the hook. I was hauled up until I was barely able to touch my toes to the floor. I was afraid at first that he was going to whip me, luckily he decided against it though.

"We will talk when I have calmed down."

I could hear him in the other room. He was pouring himself a drink. I don't know where he went after that but for now I was just grateful that he decided to punish me later. Heaven knows what he would have done to me while he was so angry.

He must have left me hanging there for at least an hour, maybe more. My shoulders ached and my wrists and back hurt. Part of me wanted him to come free me, while part of me feared what would happen when he did. Eventually he did come for me. I could tell he was still upset but the rage seemed to have died down.

After freeing me from my bonds he carried me into the bedroom and sat me down on the bed.

"Alright now, I want to hear exactly what happened this morning."

Tears pouring down my face I managed to tell him about the fit of panic and the realization that I couldn't leave him. He gave a little smile when I told him that.

"I thought perhaps you changed your mind because you realized what I might do to you when I caught you and I would have caught you."

He had a menacing look in his eyes and I could tell he was serious. There was no running away because one way or another, he would catch up with me.

"No, Master. That never crossed my mind. I stayed because I knew it was the right thing to do. It's hard to explain."

He gathered me in his arms and kissed me deeply.

"Today was intended as a test. I wanted to see how much I could trust you without supervision. Obviously you failed that test and will have to be punished, you know that don't you?"

"Yes, Master."

"However, since you came to your senses and came back of your own free will, the punishment won't be too harsh".

"Thank you, Master"

I was only just recovering from the last punishment and my ass and thighs were still sore from the cane. Now all I can do is hope that this punishment won't be as severe as the last.

"Can I trust you in the future?"

"Yes, Master."

"And I don't have to worry about you running off again?"

"No, Master. I promise it won't happen again."

"Good. I can't tell you how empty I felt when I thought you had gone."

It suddenly struck me that I felt awful not because he had hung me up or that he was going to punish me for leaving in the first place, but because I caused him pain. This was all just so confusing to me. Why did I feel this way towards him? Logically I should be angry that he was going to hurt me or that he tricked me with the tape. But logic seems to have long gone out the window when it came to how I felt about Devlin.

"Now my slave, that just leaves the matter of your punishment."

He picked up a ping pong paddle from the floor. I looked at him with some apprehension. He pulled me across his left knee, trapping my legs with his right leg, leaving me in a very vulnerable position. The first stroke of the paddle stung a lot. The second stroke brought tears to my eyes. I lost count of the number of strokes I took, but he spanked me long and hard.

My ass was burning and I was in genuine pain by the time he finally stopped and threw the paddle aside. He laid me on my stomach on the bed and ordered me not to move.

He rummaged around in the other room, before returning. I couldn't see what he had in his hand, but I felt the coldness of lotion being rubbed into my sore butt cheeks and was grateful for the relief.

Next I felt him rubbing something into my anus and before I could protest he stuck a butt plug in. It was bigger than the previous one and it didn't want to go in at first. But after more lube and some not so gentle manipulation he finally got it inside of me.

I started to protest but he stuck his fingers inside of my pussy and started to stimulate my clit. He kept stroking my clit until I fully relaxed and he was able to get the butt plug all the way inside of me.

"This is number two of five. When your body gets used to that, we'll go up to the next size. Eventually you'll be able to take the biggest."

"How big is the biggest?" I asked wearily.

"It's a step up system, one inches, two inches, three inches, four inches and the last being five. This is the only way to help your body adjust."

He tried to help me sit up but it wasn't easy with the butt plug inside of me. It was such a tight fit.

Now spread your legs," he murmured, and he helped move me towards the edge of the bed, draping my legs over the side of the mattress.

I watched with bated breath as he placed a wide lace headband over my eyes so I couldn't see what was going on. I heard the buzz of the vibrator and knew what was coming, yet I still gasped loudly when he pushed it against my labia. Delicious vibrations stimulated my clit.

"Does that feel good?"

"Yes Master," I replied breathily as the metal of the vibrator was warming my sensitive flesh.

He pushed it in deeper and my hips began to flex against the glorious device. Liquid heat surged between my thighs as the vibrator pressed against my clit. My hips thrust back and forth. It all felt so good, so hot, and so overwhelmingly delightful.

"Do you want to come?"

"Yes, Master," I panted. "So, so much."

I felt my excitement mounting by the second. The vibrator was powerful. I sat up on my knees and as Devlin thrust a finger deep inside my pussy, he growled. "Mine, all mine."

My body started to shake and tighten but Devlin left the vibrator buzzing inside of me until finally my body went limp and I fell into his arms.

I opened my eyelids sluggishly and watched in a daze as he removed the wide lace headband from my face and held me against his chest as the aftershocks of my orgasm continued to jolt through me.

He kissed my forehead while still holding me tightly in his arms.

"Don't ever try and leave me again."

Chapter 14

"Don't fall asleep my sweet slave. We don't have a lot of time before you need to start getting ready."

"What do you mean Master? Are we going somewhere?"

"We are having a client over for dinner tonight. He's very important and it's your job to keep him happy."

"Yes, Master."

Although I knew I would do what I was told, I was still worried. Did he expect me to act like some kind of high class hooker? And if he did, was I really prepared to go that far to make Devlin happy? Surely that's not what he intended.

"Exactly how far do you expect me to go to make him happy?"

He frowned at me, his mood changing instantly.

"Do you trust your Master?"

"Of course I do. I'm just …"

"You should know better than to question me."

He turned me over and started patting my bottom with his hand. It stung a bit because of the soreness from the beating I got earlier, but still it also felt a little arousing. It wasn't a brutal spanking like he has given me in the past. This spanking was more sensual than painful.

After a few strokes he put his finger in my pussy.

"Exactly what I thought. You like my hand across your ass don't you?"

"No, Master. It hurts." I tried to squirm to get away but he kept holding me down, over his knees with his finger in my pussy. I had just come so my body was still very sensitive but I enjoyed having his finger inside of me.

"Liar. Your body tells me exactly what I need to know about you. Look how wet your pussy is. I should fuck you good and hard, right here and now."

He was right. I was turned on and more than anything I wanted him to fuck me.

As he fingered my clit, the lips of my pussy swelled and yearned for him to give me more. He kept at it until I was a mass of quivering nerves. I moaned and pushed myself against his hand. But as I was just about to come he pulled away. I could barely breathe. I wanted him so bad. I wanted his cock inside of me.

He sat me up on his lap and I started to grind against him. As we kissed I tugged at his shirt, to get him to remove it. I wanted to put my hands all over his rock hard abs. When he removed his shirt, I melted into him and let him hold me tight against his body.

"I need you," I breathed.

And that was all it took. He threw me down on the bed and I landed on my stomach. I heard him unzip his pants and a few moments later I felt his hands on my hips.

I gasped as he entered me from behind. He slid forward slowly, inch by inch. He was barely moving, and I wanted to scream for him to hurry. I so desperately wanted all of him inside of me.

He started to move deeper into me and my body felt so completely filled. He pulled out of me and the head of his cock rested at my opening. I felt the emptiness it left behind, my sensitive flesh throbbing, immediately wanting to be filled again.

I thrust my hips backwards, forcing him back inside of me. The fullness, the way he stretched me, was all building and spiraling inside of me towards an orgasm. I closed my eyes and focused on the sensation of his cock inside of me.

His thick cock drove brutally into me, pushing me over the edge. He slammed into me again and again before he groaned loudly. I felt his cock twitch and jerk inside me.

My own orgasm ripped through me, gripping my entire body, making me arch and twist, moving my hips back and forth on his spurting cock as he pushed hard inside of me, as deep as it would go.

He stayed inside of me while we both recovered. Very slowly he pulled out of me and I took in a deep shuddering breath. I hated how it felt when he pulled out of me. I loved the intimate feeling of having him inside of me. I loved how it united us as one.

I rolled on my back and my legs felt so weak and limp. I have been truly and thoroughly fucked and I had no idea how I was going to have the strength to get out of bed and be a good hostess for his client tonight.

I wanted to fall asleep in Devlin's arms but just as I started to doze off I heard the doorbell ring. My head shot up and I started to panic. Devlin just laughed.

"Don't worry. It's just Olga and Anika here to clean the house."

I looked at him in confusion and he continued.

"Olga and Anika are my housekeepers. I gave them the last few weeks off to give us some alone time. Now go get in the shower and get ready while I go get the door."

When I got out of the shower, and fixed my hair and makeup, I found the clothes that Devlin had laid out for me to wear on the bed. Tonight I would be wearing the black and white corset with matching black and white tutu. Luckily he set out some panties for me as well, the tutu was far too short to not have something on underneath.

I loved the way the corset pushed up my boobs making me look like I had far more upstairs than I really did. I pranced into the kitchen feeling so pretty to get Devlin's approval and found him making finger foods.

"You still aren't ready yet?" I asked him. "Let me finish these while you go get in the shower."

Devlin turned his head and looked at me. When he did, a big smile came across his face and I knew he liked how I looked.

I kissed his cheek and took over making the hors d'oeuvres while he went to shower, shave and put his suit on.

I just finished sprinkling olive oil on the final tray of bruschetta when the doorbell rang. I organized the grilled scallops wrapped in prosciutto with the spicy tuna tartar while Devlin answered the door. I came in just after holding the first tray of finger foods.

"Mr. Ryland this is Mary Elizabeth."

"Please call me Jamison."

I curtsied and gave him my best coy smile. "It's so wonderful to meet you Jamison. Please come in and take a seat."

I gestured towards the couch and he took a seat while Devlin sat in the chair next to him. I sat the tray of food down in front of them on the coffee table and went to get the tray of lobster sliders with cheesy stuffed mushrooms.

When I walked out of the room I heard them making small talk. After setting the next tray of food down I went to get the wine.

I handed the bottle to Devlin along with the opener. "It looks like we'll be having a 2008 Col Solare tonight."

When he popped the cork on the wine bottle it fell to the floor. Without thinking I bent over Devlin's lap to grab it and when I did, our guest had the perfect view of my ass. My skirt was just so short, he could probably see everything. When I heard him let out a quiet moan, I knew exactly what I had done. I jumped up and went back to serving them finger foods and wine.

As I bent over to pour the wine in his glass, the man didn't take his eyes off of my chest and Devlin was the one getting an eyeful of my ass. For some reason he decided to stick his finger in my pussy just as I was bent over Jamison with the bottle of wine. I squealed and jumped and when I did I spilled wine on the poor man. I grabbed some napkins and immediately started to clean it up, apologizing to Jamison profusely.

I was so worried about apologizing to him and cleaning up my mess, I didn't think about where exactly it was my hands were rubbing.

"Mary Elizabeth, it's fine," Devlin said as he pulled me away.

"I'm so sorry. I can't believe I did that."

"It's okay sweetie. Go into the kitchen and check on things. I'll call for you if we need you."

I did as I was told and went into the kitchen and pulled myself together. I sat at the table and waited for

Devlin to call for me. When he did this time, it was to bring in the 2010 Duhart Milon that he set out earlier. It's an expensive Bordeaux.

I poured the first glass for Jamison and he still couldn't take his eyes off of my breasts. When I turned around to pour a glass for Devlin, again I knew my ass was in Jamison's face. I hate to admit it, but I liked knowing he was turned on by me. But what I wasn't expecting was for him to reach up and gently stroke my ass. He didn't even know me and he had his hand on me. Who just touches someone they don't even know like that? I hope he doesn't think this thing is going to go any further. I only touched Jamison's cock by accident. I was trying to clean up the wine I spilled on him. It wasn't meant to be a sexual thing.

Devlin pulled me down on his lap and sipped his wine. Jamison downed his glass and then excused himself to go to the restroom. When he stood up to go, I couldn't help but notice the tent in his pants and I knew exactly what he was going to do in there.

The second the bathroom door was shut, Devlin put his hand between my legs and forcefully pressed his finger inside of me.

"I see someone is enjoying themselves."

I squirmed on his lap, trying to get him to pull his finger out of my pussy but he kept thrusting his finger in and out of my pussy forcefully.

"Don't act so shy now," he admonished. "You've been showing your ass all night so maybe you would like to spread your legs for him too."

"Master no, the only person I want to share my body with is you."

I really thought that Devlin was just teasing me but when he ordered me to go to my room and wait for him to call for me, I knew he was serious.

As I walked away, Jamison came out of the bathroom. Man he was fast. Oh God, why did I just think of the man playing with his cock in our bathroom? What is wrong with me?

I don't know how long the two of them spent talking in the living room, but it felt like forever. With every long minute that passed I began to dread what awaited me later that night.

After a while, I poked my head out of my bedroom door and overheard them speaking.

"Mr. Kent I must say, your little Mary Elizabeth has to be one of the hottest girls I've ever seen. When she popped out of that kitchen in that little getup, I couldn't believe my eyes."

Devlin chuckled. "Yes, I am a lucky man."

"Seeing how devoted that lovely girl is to you, makes me realize I've made the right decision to give my business to you and your firm."

The two continued their conversation for a few more minutes before I heard the main door open and close so I hurried back to sit back down on the bed and wait for Devlin to call for me. It wasn't long before he came into my room. I looked up from reading my book and seen him leaning against the door frame, just watching me.

"I see you enjoyed yourself tonight."

"What do you mean Master?"

"I mean, you seemed to enjoy showing your ass to our guest."

"No Master. It wasn't like that at all."

I jumped out of the bed and ran to Devlin and put my hands on his chest and pleaded with him to understand it wasn't anything I did intentionally. It was all just a horrible series of missteps and mistakes.

"Don't tell me you didn't enjoy having him stare at your tits when you poured his glass of wine or how hard you made his dick when you bent over and showed him your ass several times throughout the night."

"No Master, please. I didn't. You are the only person I want to show my body to. You have to believe me."

"That's the problem. I don't believe you. I felt your pussy. I know exactly how turned on you were tonight. You know damn well you liked showing that man your ass."

Tears started to form in my eyes.

"Did it get you all hot and bothered knowing that he was so worked up over looking at your body he had to go to the bathroom and relieve himself? You had him so turned on he couldn't even wait until he left to play with his cock."

"Devlin please, I'm serious. All playing around aside, I would never ever in a million years want some strange man I don't even know touching me. You don't understand. I'm not that kind of girl. I haven't …."

"Apparently we need to find a better way to remind you that your body is mine. You belong to me."

I lifted my wrist, showing him my tattoo.

"I don't need another reminder. I already know that I'm yours forever and always and I wouldn't want it any other way."

He grabbed my wrist tightly and lifted it up.

"Clearly this marking isn't enough."

He has a bizarre look in his eyes, almost crazed.

"Please Devlin, you are really hurting me," I cried out as I tried to pull my wrist back but he wasn't letting me go.

Devlin was angry and this didn't bode well for me or my ass which was still tender from all the previous spankings.

"Come with me," he commanded. As he pulled me out to the living room, grabbing my leash and snapping it in place before dragging me out the front door and to his car.

I had no idea where we were headed and I was quite frankly too afraid to ask. I sat quietly in the passenger's seat as he drove into the night.

After a while I finally got up the nerve to ask.

"Where are we headed Master?"

"We are going to the club. Maybe there are some people there you would like to show your ass to. Or maybe you can stick your perfect little tits in their face and see if you can make their dicks hard too."

I wasn't expecting him to take me to the club. I couldn't help but start to panic as I wondered what he had in mind for me there. When we entered, we made our way through the first bar area, and then instead of turning towards the grand ballroom we went into last time, he took me in the opposite direction.

Unlike before, the bar area this time was packed. There were at least thirty or more people sitting around the small tables having drinks. I couldn't really see any of their faces, to know if I recognized any of them from before, because I was being dragged off into another room.

Strangely, none of the other patrons in the bar even seemed to notice Devlin pulling me along by my leash. If I was sitting in a bar and seen some pissed off man dragging a girl into a back room, I think at the very least I would turn my head to watch. But not here, these people just acted as if this was an everyday occurrence to them -- Maybe it was.

Devlin's anger hadn't dissipated and I feared finding out what he had in mind for me. Was he planning on giving me another tattoo, marking me as his, like he had done before? Did he plan on inking my butt cheeks this time or maybe my breasts? But if that was his plan, why bring me here to his club instead of the tattoo parlor that we went to last time?

"Come," he said as he led me into a room towards the back. It was dimly lit with medieval looking furnishings. There were pieces of equipment scattered around the room. I had no idea what they were for, but they all looked designed to cause pain.

"This is the dungeon. It's where we bring very naughty slaves."

It was then I noticed the men wearing black leather masks. One was locked in a cage, while another was strung up, against the wall. Neither men had any clothes on, other than the black leather masks.

The room was lit with primitive looking torches with real fire. There didn't seem to be a modern day light bulb in the entire room. In fact there didn't seem to be much of anything modern in there. I began to grow afraid.

"Why did you bring me in here Master?"

He didn't respond. He just kept guiding me towards the corner of the room. He stood in front of what appeared to be a padded table that was about three feet high.

"Bend over the table," he commanded.

I was scared just being in this room. I could only imagine the pain he could inflict upon my body in here.

"Please Master, I'm sorry."

"Bend over the table," he repeated.

Reluctantly, I did as he asked. He fastened wrist and ankle cuffs on me and then tied me down securely by means of hooks set in the top and legs of the table. I couldn't move any part of my body. He had me locked down good with my ass exposed for what I only assumed was going to be a severe beating.

I heard him searching for something. When he found it, he held it up in front of my face but to my surprise, it wasn't a whip.

It was a long slim rod of metal with something on the end. It was dim in there and I couldn't quite make out what it was. He brought it closer and I could see it was a rod with an initial "D" on one end. It looked like, but could surely not be, a branding iron similar to one I had seen on a farm once. Surely that wasn't what it was though. He couldn't possibly plan on branding me like cattle. I had teased him about doing such a thing once before, but fuck, I had no idea he would ever really consider it.

"Yes my dear, it's what you think it is." He paused to smooth my hair back from my forehead. "It's a branding iron and after I use this on you there will be no more question of whom you belong to."

On dear God, he really does intend to use that on me.

Devlin walked over to a fire pit that was in front of me and using one of the torches lit it up. He put the iron in the fire to heat it up. I wondered how often those irons had been used. He must have read my mind because he said "You'd be surprised how often this form of punishment is used."

I couldn't believe he was going to brand me. I was terrified. I cried and begged and pleaded for him not to do this to me. He paid no attention.

"This room is sound proofed so feel free to scream if it hurts, because nobody will hear you"

At last the brand was heated to his satisfaction and he showed it to me. It was glowing red hot. He put the brand back in the fire while he chose a place on my ass to place the brand.

I was unable to move at all and there was nothing I could do to stop Devlin from doing this. He approached with the iron and without hesitating brought it down on my right ass cheek. I screamed as I felt it searing my flesh, burning his initial there for all time.

The pain was overwhelming and more than I could take. I felt dizzy and suddenly the room was spinning. The pain in my ass cheek was so piercing that I struggled to breath.

Devlin put the iron in a nearby bucket of water and I heard this hissing sound it made as it heated up the water. He left me lying there across the table while I struggled to not pass out.

For a moment there was a flash of light as the door opened. Whoever it was began to talk to Devlin but I couldn't make out what they were saying. I couldn't focus on anything at that moment except for the pain.

Whoever this person was laid a tender hand on my forehead. It was then I realized the person was a female. I couldn't make out what she looked like but I smelt the faint scent of her perfume along with the gentle way she touched me and I just knew.

She walked around to the back of the table and took a good look at my ass. "Well, you've done a proper job at least. That will heal nicely. You wouldn't believe the mess some people make trying to brand a slave."

I don't know which one of them did it, but one of them began to pour cool water over my skin. While it felt good, I could still feel a burning sensation, so I knew my skin was still being burned. I was desperate for relief. This really was going to scar me for life.

"Here try this," I heard the feminine voice say to Devlin.

I couldn't see what it was she had in her hand but she gave him something wrapped in a towel. A few seconds later he placed a cold compress on my burn. Finally I was getting some much needed relief. I had no idea who this woman was, but I was grateful for her help.

Devlin undid my restraints and helped me to stand up. I didn't have the strength to stand on my own so he lifted me in his arms. It was then I got my first look at the lady who had been speaking with Devlin.

"Well hello there," she said tenderly.

"This is Mistress Sophie," Devlin whispered in my ear.

"Take this," she said as she put some pills in my mouth and held a glass of water up to help me wash them down. I didn't know what it was she gave me, I assume it was some ibuprofen to help with the pain.

Mistress Sophie was tiny. She couldn't possibly stand more than five feet tall and weigh more than ninety pounds soaking wet. She had long blonde hair with big green eyes that seemed so full of life. Her skin was pale, and clear, like porcelain. But most captivating about her was her smile. It was so big, beautiful and warm, you just had to smile back at her.

For some reason I thought all female Dom's had jet black hair bright red lips and matching long, bright red nails. But Mistress Sophie wasn't your stereotypical dominatrix. Even her clothes were unique. She wore a floor length sheer backless gown with an extremely high cut slit that went all the way up her side.

I was too weak to say anything to her, but I couldn't stop staring at her. She was beautiful and captivating. I was looking into her eyes when the room began to spin again and I passed out.

Chapter 15

When I woke up we were back at Devlin's penthouse and I was safely tucked into my bed, lying on my stomach. Devlin was standing over me, rubbing some sort of gel into my burn. I didn't say anything. I was still upset. I couldn't believe he branded me. The tattoo was one thing, but this was just too much.

A single tear rolled down my face. I tried my best to control my emotions. I didn't want to start balling because I didn't want Devlin to know I was awake. I didn't want to talk to him. I didn't want to see him. I didn't want him to touch me.

I heard the doorbell ring and Devlin went to greet whoever it was. I couldn't tell who it was at first but I could hear Devlin speaking to them.

"Yes, it was harsh but she needs to learn."

I couldn't make out what the other person said in response to Devlin but I could tell by his voice that he seemed annoyed with whoever it was.

"Yes, but I fully intend on keeping this one forever. She's not just a passing fancy." He said something else I couldn't understand and then asked if whoever was at the door would like to see me.

When they entered my room I could smell the scent of Mistress Sophie's perfume and I knew it was her. I couldn't see her face because I was lying on my stomach but I turned my head to see her as she sat down on the side of the bed.

"I'll leave you two alone," Devlin said as he walked out of the room closing the door behind him.

I rolled on my side carefully and Mistress Sophie helped me prop myself up on my elbow so we could speak.

"How are you feeling?" She asked as she cleared the hair off of my forehead.

"Tired and weak. I still feel totally out of it too, like my brain is foggy."

"That's probably just the pain killers."

Mistress Sophie stroked my forehead. She had such a soothing, gentle touch.

"I remember the first time I seen you at the club with Master D. I knew you were something special."

"It was before my initiation, right?"

"Yes, I was there that night. I didn't participate in your initiation though. I was busy with my own slave. But still, I knew there something about you and that one day we would be friends."

"Is your slave a female? I don't remember meeting your slave."

"No, I've never had a female slave before."

"Have you known Master D for a long time?" I asked.

"I suppose I have. I met him years ago, but we typically run in different circles."

She put her hand on my hip and I winced.

"Are you still in a lot of pain sweetie?"

"Yes, I am. The type of pain changes. Like right now it's a dull throbbing pain. It's bearable but still pretty intense."

Just then Devlin came into the room to check on us.

"When's the last time she's had some pain pills? She's still in a lot of pain."

"It's been awhile. She has been asleep for the last twelve hours. I thought it was better to let her rest than to wake her up just to give her more pain meds that will only make her want to sleep more."

"I agree. That's probably a good choice."

Devlin came over to the side of the bed and took the pills out of the bottle on the nightstand. He put them in my mouth and helped me drink some water to wash them down.

"You know Master D, I was thinking, I would like to come back tomorrow and check on our little patient and maybe fix her room up a bit. Give it a more feminine touch. That is if you don't mind."

"What do you think Mary Elizabeth? Would you like Mistress Sophie to fix your room up for you?"

"I think that whatever you want is fine with me Master. I only want to please you."

Devlin gave me an indulgent smile and then turned his attention to Mistress Sophie.

"So what exactly did you have in mind?"

"I don't know, nothing drastic. Just a few flowers and maybe paintings. Just something to give the room a more feminine feel."

"I have to work tomorrow afternoon. Maybe you can come by then and take care of Mary Elizabeth and do your thing then?"

"That sounds great. I'll be here around noon."

As Mistress Sophie was leaving my eyes became heavy and I felt myself falling asleep. I tried my best to fight it. I wanted to talk to Devlin about what happened but in the end sleep won out.

By the time I woke up the next day Mistress Sophie had come and gone. When I opened my eyes I took in the new decorations in my room. She replaced the ceiling fan with a beautiful crystal chandelier. Instead of the boring mini-blinds from before, the windows now had flowing drapes that perfectly matched my new bedspread and the rug at the foot of my bed. On my nightstand was a beautiful arrangement of fresh flowers and above my headboard where three large paintings, side by side.

I hate that I slept through all of it and didn't get a chance to thank her. I hoped that she would return soon so I could show her my sincere appreciation for her decorating skills.

I heard some clanging noises coming from the other room and then was distracted with the smell of maple syrup. My stomach started growling and I crawled out to the kitchen to see what it was Devlin was cooking.

Devlin told me to get up and take a seat at the table. I did so very carefully, sitting on the edge of the chair, careful not to let the chair scrape against my still very tender skin. He put a stack of pancakes in front of me. I was so hungry and devoured everything on my plate.

"You are such an amazing cook Master. These are without a doubt the best pancakes I've ever had. They are so light and fluffy."

"It's nice to have someone to cook for."

When Devlin got up and put my dishes in the sink, the doorbell rang and I caught him rolling his. He mumbled something under his breath and then went to answer the door.

I ran to my bedroom because I didn't have any clothes on and didn't want whoever it was at the door to come into the kitchen and see me sitting there at the table completely naked. As I was throwing on a t-shirt I overheard Devlin telling Mistress Sophie that I was in my room. Before long she came in pulling her slave on a leash behind her.

Mistress Sophie was very tiny so the last thing I expected was her to have a slave that was well over six foot tall and weighed probably two hundred and fifty pounds. He was a big guy, and I mean linebacker big. It was a sight to see this mammoth of a man follow around such a tiny little Sophie like a love sick puppy.

"There's my baby girl. How are we feeling today?"

"Much better Mistress Sophie. I love what you did to my room. It's all so beautiful."

She waved it off. "Don't be silly. It was nothing."

I looked up at her slave. "Who is your friend?"

Mistress Sophie tugged on his leash and he stepped forward. "This is my new toy. Isn't he dreamy?"

We both giggled as he stood there at attention, waiting for Mistress Sophie to address him.

Devlin entered the room and Mistress Sophie's entire demeanor changed. There really was some strange tension between her and Devlin and I had no idea why.

"Well I better be heading out now. Slave and I were just heading out to the club and I wanted to stop by on the way to see what you thought of your new room."

She leaned over and kissed my cheek and then Devlin showed her out. After Devlin returned to my room.

"I don't recall giving you permission to get dressed."

"I'm sorry Master. It won't happen again."

"Remove those clothes."

I took off my t-shirt and then my panties. I noticed Devlin watching me carefully. He seemed to really enjoy watching me undress.

"Why don't you like Mistress Sophie?"

Devlin chuckled. "What makes you think that?"

"I saw the look on your face when the doorbell rang. I also remember the first night I met her, at the club. You didn't seem the slightest bit interested in speaking with her, like you did others."

He sighed. "Let's just say that Mistress Sophie and I are two very different people."

"What do you mean? You seem to get along well enough with other Dom's from the club. Why not her?"

"It's not that I dislike her per say. Mistress Sophie comes from a very wealthy family, one of the most powerful oil families in the entire state of Texas. When Sophie turned eighteen her family married her off to the son from a family in Venezuela with large oil holdings."

I gasped. I couldn't believe that Mistress Sophie was married.

"From what I understand the couple has never spent more than a few days together. He stayed in South America with his mistress and she stayed in Texas, choosing instead to entertain herself with a stable of slave boys."

"A stable? I thought you said a Master only ever has one slave."

"That's true for a male Master with a female slave. It's an issue of trust. There is a very special relationship between a Master and a slave. But when it comes to female Dom's and male slaves, the psychological makeup is different. The need for fidelity isn't ingrained into the male psyche in the same way that it is in the female brain. So while it's not common, it is perfectly acceptable for a female Dom to have more than one slave as long as she is able to provide for all of their needs."

"Does Mistress Sophie still keep a stable of slaves or does she just have the one now?"

"I think she just keeps one for now. But she doesn't seem to keep one for any length of time. She gets bored quickly and moves on from one to the next."

"Is that why you don't like her Master, because she's flighty?"

"It's not that I don't like her, I just don't know that she's necessarily a good influence on you. She seems to be fixated on you though, so I don't think she'll be going away anytime soon."

I put my arms around Devlin's neck and played with the back of his hair.

"I like her Master. She's pretty and it's fun to have another female to talk to. Maybe the three of us could do that thing we talked about before?"

Devlin looked at me quizzically, perhaps trying to remember what it was I was talking about.

"Oh no, no. It doesn't work that way. Two Dom's together is a bad idea. Trust me when I say, someone like Mistress Sophie doesn't do it for me in the slightest. If you want to play I'll find you a toy, but not Mistress Sophie. You can play with her if you want though. I don't mind if you are with other women."

I stood up on my tippy toes, pulling his face down to mine and kissed Devlin.

"I don't need any new toys Master. All I need is you."

I dropped down to my knees and unzipped his pants. His cock had a drop of fluid on the slit and I took great pleasure in licking it off as I took it out from the confines of his pants.

I wrapped my lips around his cock and sucked vigorously. I leaned forward, taking in as much as I could. He put his hands on the back of my head, threading his fingers in my hair and pulling me into him.

I felt his hardened cock slipping through my parted lips and hitting the back of my throat. I grabbed his balls with one hand, while stroking his cock with the other. His breathing was short and furious so I pulled back, not wanting him to come just yet.

I slid my tongue slowly down his length. I put his cock back in my mouth, sucking enthusiastically and his hips moved as if they were on fire before he finally exploded into my mouth.

Chapter 16

"Come with me," Devlin said as he led me into his office in his penthouse.

I'd only seen the room once or twice before. He usually kept it locked up. He motioned for me to sit down at his desk. When I did he opened his laptop and then clicked on the icon for the email program. When it opened I notice it was my email that he had loaded up. I looked up at him, wondering what it was he wanted me to do.

"You have some messages I want you to respond to. Your sister has sent you a few emails and is worried about you and there are a few from some of the ladies in the office. I want you to let them know you are okay."

"Yes, Master."

I clicked on the emails from my sister and read them. They were mostly just updates about her dogs. She sent several pictures of them dressed up in various outfits and then told me about some of the things they have been doing. She seriously loves those dogs way too much.

I typed up my replies to each of the emails, keeping what I had to say light and casual. I decided not to mention Devlin and instead just said that I was doing well and had been so busy lately with work.

The next email I read was from Corbin Tedlow. He was just touching base with me from the last time we ran into each other and wanted to know what was going on with me and Devlin. He didn't know we were a thing and he demanded I fill him in on all the juicy details. I had to laugh. That's so Corbin.

Devlin who was still standing over my shoulder reading every word I read and wrote, just grunted, clearly not happy about my friendship with Corbin.

I replied to Corbin's email as well as a few others from some of the girls, letting them all know I was doing well and missed them so much and said that I hoped to see them soon. If nothing else, maybe we could all do lunch sometime.

"I wrote a letter for you to send. You'll find it in the draft folder."

I clicked on the email he was speaking of and read it. It was an email to Mr. Moretti thanking him for the opportunity to work for Ashworth and Kent but letting them know I was quitting.

"I have bills. If I quit my job how am I supposed to pay them?"

"I told you Mary Elizabeth, I will take care of you. That means provide for you in every way including paying your bills, providing for a roof over your head, food in your stomach and new clothes."

I couldn't believe Devlin was making me quit my job. I guess if I really thought about it, I was probably about to be fired anyway since I had been gone so long but still, this was really just so overwhelming. Plus I had several credit cards. Surely he doesn't intend on paying those off.

"I have credit card debt Master. I can't ask you to pay those off."

"I've taken care of that already."

"All of them Master?"

Yes. Now let's drop the subject. I told you I would take care of you and that means your past debts, and all future purchases."

"Thank you, Master. That's so generous of you."

I turned back to the laptop, put a few personal touches on my resignation email and then pressed send. I would miss some of my co-workers but I knew this was the right thing to do, especially if I wanted my relationship with Devlin to work.

During the next two weeks Devlin made extra effort to take care of me while my body recovered from the branding. When he worked from home he let me come into his office and help. It was nice to feel needed. Devlin was always doing so much for me, I loved that he let me finally do something for him.

After a few hours of filing Devlin sat back in his chair and smiled at me. He seemed to take extra pleasure in watching me bend over and organize his files.

"You getting hungry?"

"Yes Master, I really am. What are we having for lunch?"

"I haven't given it much thought. You hungry for anything special?"

"You know Master, I could whip us up something while you finish going through those contracts. I know you still have a lot of work to do."

"That sounds good. Let me know if you need help with anything."

I went into the kitchen and started going through the cabinets and refrigerator to see what I could come up with to make us for lunch. I wasn't exactly the best cook so I needed to find something simple that still tasted delicious.

I decided to make grilled chicken salad. It wasn't fancy but it would do. After lunch Devlin informed me that he had to go to the office to drop off the contracts and find some missing paperwork for an important client. He wasn't sure how long he would be gone but that Mistress Sophie would be stopping by to keep me company.

I was excited to see Mistress Sophie, it had been awhile since her last visit.

Devlin was distracted with work so after lunch I did the dishes and let him get back to his contracts.

Afterwards I sat down on the floor next to Devlin while he worked, to quietly read a book on the Kindle Devlin had bought me from Amazon. It was a romance novella about a girl who was in love with her best friend's older brother.

Just as I finished the doorbell rang and Devlin ordered me to answer it. I looked down at my completely naked body and looked back at Devlin pleadingly.

"I said go answer it."

"Yes, Master."

I got up and did as I was told. Still, I was mortified. I couldn't believe he was going to make me answer the door without my clothes on. I worried who would be at the door. It was still far too early for it to be Mistress Sophie, she wasn't due for another hour.

It could be anyone on the other side of that door and they were about to see my naked body. I was freaking out on my way to answer the door, hoping whoever it was would walk away before I got there. I however wouldn't be so lucky and had to open the door and face whoever it was.

I opened the door and on the other side was Mistress Sophie. She was early and I was relieved. She let her gaze run down my body and a big smile came across her face.

"Well, well, what do we have here?"

I opened the door all of the way and ushered her and her slave inside.

"Hello Mistress Sophie. You are early today."

"Yes baby girl, I am. I couldn't wait to see you." She handed me a stack of DVDs. "I picked out some movies we could watch tonight. Pick your favorite."

I plopped down on the couch while looking through the stack of movies she brought and Mistress Sophie took a seat next to me. Her slave stood in the corner as he always did, waiting to be called upon. It was amazing the self-control he had. I don't think I've ever heard him say a single thing except "Yes, Mistress" or "No, Mistress".

The movies she brought where all romantic comedies, something I never got to watch with Devlin. I decided on 'Ever After' with Drew Barrymore. As I sat it down on the coffee table Devlin came out of his office to greet Mistress Sophie. He glanced down at the stack of movies and rolled his eyes.

"I'm glad you are early. I need to get to the office. Will you girls be okay while I'm gone?"

I jumped up and kissed his cheek. "We'll be fine Master. Don't worry about us."

As soon as Devlin left, Mistress Sophie and I turned on the movie. I don't know what it was about being with Sophie but I like having her around. She just had a way of putting me at ease.

We cuddled together on the sofa watching the movie when for some reason my eyes drifted over to her slave standing in the corner of the room.

He wore a collar like I did, only his was wider. The first time I met him he wore a leather Gladiator kilt. With his muscular build, it was pretty sexy. Last time he had on black sheer boxer briefs but tonight he wore nothing but a black leather harness across his chest.

His cock was tied up with what looked like a thick black leather strap. It was just hanging out there in the open all floppy. I don't know what came over me but I couldn't help but want to smack it and see if it moved. Thinking about it made me giggle and when I did I caught Mistress Sophie's attention.

"What's so funny?"

"I was just thinking about your slave. What's his name?"

"He doesn't have a name, other than slave boy."

"He never talks. How in the world do you get him to stand there quietly for so long? He's like one of those guards in London who stand in front of the palace and no matter what you do or say they don't move or show facial expressions."

Mistress Sophie choked back a laugh.

"I don't know about that but he is a former member of the military special ops force and he knows better. He is not to speak until spoken to, unlike you. You are so lucky your master won't let me punish you. I would love to get my hands on that sweet little ass of yours."

Mistress Sophie rolled me on her stomach and ran her hand over my bare ass. Her touch was gentle and erotic.

Before I knew what was happening she flipped me back over and had put a finger inside of me and began stroking my clit. It felt so amazing and I soon found myself lost in the sensation of her touch.

"You need to learn to let go Mary Elizabeth."

I didn't understand what she meant by that. Let go of what?

"It's one thing to say you embrace the lifestyle. But if you ever want to be truly happy with Master D then you need to let go of your fears and inhibitions and learn to just be free. You need to learn to trust him, truly trust him or you'll never find that peace and happiness you want with him."

She leaned in to kiss me while she continued to tease my pussy with her fingers. The feel of her velvety, moist tongue in my mouth had me aching with desire.

"Do you love Master D?"

"Yes I do, with all of my heart."

"Then stop worrying about what other people think or what might be right or wrong. Just be with him and trust that he will always take care of you. Until you can learn to do that, you will never be truly happy."

What she said made sense. I guess I hadn't really thought about that before now.

"If you worry too much about what others think is right or wrong, you will always be a prisoner to their feelings and their way of doing things. You have to live for yourself and for your love of your Master. If he tells you to walk to the door naked, like he did today, you can trust that it will be okay. It doesn't matter who the person is on the other side of the door or what they may think when you open the door and stand before them with no clothes on. All that matters is your love and trust of Master D. You deserve to be happy, so be happy. Trust he will take care of you."

"I do trust him."

"Don't just say the words, really mean them. If you really trusted him then you wouldn't have been so scared to answer the door when I came over today. I seen the look of relief on your face when you opened the door and saw it was me."

"You are right Mistress Sophie. I was worried about answering the door."

"Don't let fear decide your future. Accept what is meant to be with Master D and let go of all the rest. Just have faith in your love for him."

"How do I do that?"

"After my marriage I was really in a bad place. I didn't like him, he didn't like me. I just wanted to end it all. But then I met someone who helped me through it. She taught me that to be truly happy I had to find the courage to let go of what I can't change. You can't change the fact that Master D made you answer the door naked, so just own it. Put the fear out of your mind and know that whatever you are doing, Master D would never hurt you, not really. You don't need the person on the other side of the door to validate you. Who cares if someone sees you naked? All that you care about is making Master D happy and if answering the door naked makes him happy, then that is all that should matter to you."

As I was giving thought to what she said, Mistress Sophie repositioned herself so that she was able to slide her tongue down from my belly button to my pussy, until she found my sweet spot. I was shaking with anticipation of that tongue's arrival to its final destination.

She ran her tongue along the length of my folds and then flicked her tongue in and out like a serpent. My entire body shook and I rocked my hips against her mouth as she devoured my swollen clit.

She flicked and licked me for a while, rotating form slow to fast strokes. She replaced her tongue with a finger, making little circles and then returned her tongue to my clit, licking steadily.

It was the most amazing feeling. I loved how it felt being with Devlin, but this was different, so sensual, so tender. She continued licking as my body tensed and trembled. I found myself grinding down hard on her mouth as my body rived in ecstasy. My juices were flowing from her chin as she stood up, walked over to her slave and kissed him passionately.

"Do you like how she tastes?" Mistress Sophie asked him.

"Yes, Mistress."

Mistress Sophie picked up her riding crop and smacked his cock hard. I could hear the noise he made. I felt bad for him but I knew better than to interfere.

"Did you enjoy watching me make her come?"

Slave boy's eyes flashed quickly from her face to the riding crop. She tapped it lightly against her leg to get his attention.

"Yes, Mistress."

She brought the tip of the crop underneath his chin.

"Do you want to fuck her?"

"No, Mistress. My cock is only for you."

She swatted his balls hard and he grunted. I wondered if she would fuck him and let me watch. I don't know what my obsession is with watching but I really wanted to see them having sex.

I noticed the strap wrapped around his cock was moving, struggling to maintain his erection. I couldn't stop looking. I knew it was probably wrong of me to stare at this guy's cock but I couldn't force myself to look away. It just kept growing and growing right before my eyes. His cock wasn't huge like Devlin's was, but it was still a sight to see. It was like the harder he struggled to maintain his composure the harder he got.

"I was going to let you pleasure me but now I just don't know."

Mistress Sophie finally noticed his ill-advised erection and her beautiful face clouded with anger.

"Listen to me you pathetic piece of shit. What the fuck did I tell you about letting your cock get hard without permission?"

"I'm sorry, Mistress."

"You are sorry? If you were sorry you wouldn't have done it in the first place. Get on your knees."

Mistress Sophie wore very high heeled, platform boots, something I always assumed she did to give her extra height since she was so tiny. Now however I see there was another reason, and that was to inflict pain on her slave. She stepped down on his shoulder, forcing it to the ground so that his butt was now higher in the air.

The riding crop came down on his ass several times. Then she changed positions, spreading her legs apart and standing over him. He lifted his head up and started licking her pussy.

I couldn't make myself look away if I had to. It was all just so incredibly hot.

As her moans became louder I could tell she was close to orgasm. But much to my surprise she didn't let him finish. She pushed him onto his back. Her slave was a big man, and she was really tiny so anything she did to him, it was only because he let her. So when I say she pushed him back, it was more like, he let her push him onto the floor.

She sat on his chest. "Is your cock hard for me?" She asked as she reached her hands behind her, working skillfully to free it from the leather straps that bound it together.

After it was free, he sat up, with Mistress Sophie still on his lap. She leaned in and kissed him passionately.

"My cock is always hard for you Mistress." The way he said it was more than an answer to her question, it was erotic and passionate, almost loving.

He lifted her tiny body up and sat her down on his cock. As the two of them had sex in front of me I noticed a strong connection between them, a truly intimate one.

Mistress Sophie may deny it, but I think she really has feelings for him and watching the two of them connect in this way, right in front of me, I could see it. That's just not something you can fake.

After it was over she made her slave go to the kitchen and clean up in the sink while Mistress Sophie and I went to shower together. Since we were truly alone, I had to ask about her husband.

"Mistress Sophie are you really married to some guy you haven't seen in years?"

"Yes, my husband lives in Santa Ana De Coro, Venezuela. Or at least the last I heard that is where he was staying with his lover."

"Why do you stay married to him if you never see him or apparently even speak to him?"

"It's a complicated family issue. I don't really want to get into it. Let's just say it's for everyone's best interest that I remain married to Santos."

"Don't you want to fall in love and have children one day?"

Mistress Sophie laughed. "Not every girl wants the white picket fence fantasy."

"You are so absolutely beautiful Mistress Sophie. I just want to see you happy."

"Oh baby girl, I am happy. I really am. I have a great life. It may not be the traditional one that most have but I think I have it even better."

After getting out of the shower, she did my hair and makeup so that I would be ready for when Devlin got back home. Then we went back to sit on the couch and watched the rest of our movie.

Her slave stood back in his corner, looking off into the distance as he always did, never making eye contact and not speaking unless spoken to.

While we watched the rest of the movie I began to think about what she said about letting go of my fears and trusting in Devlin. She was right, it's easy to say you love someone, but it's another thing all together to really mean it.

My grandmother always used to say that the best way to feel happy is to make other people you care about happy. I always thought that was silly. But now I do truly get what she meant by that. I want to make Devlin happy. I want to be good for him. I want to submit to him in every way. I will learn to let go, somehow.

I heard the familiar click and clang of the elevator door and jumped up to greet Devlin as he entered the living room.

"I missed you Master, welcome home."

He leaned down and kissed my forehead and he shut the door behind him. He handed me his briefcase and I ran to put it in his office as he took his seat in the living room.

"Would you like a drink Master?"

"No, I'm fine," he said as he patted his knee indicating he wanted me to come sit on his lap.

"Were you a good girl while I was gone?"

"Yes, Master I was a very good girl."

He looked towards Mistress Sophie. "I hope she wasn't too much trouble for you."

"Not at all Master D. She was quite the good little girl in your absence."

I giggled.

"You going to that thing tomorrow at the club?" Mistress Sophie asked Devlin.

"Yes, I wouldn't miss it. How often do you get the chance to meet an actual Prince?" Devlin replied sarcastically.

Something in his tone told me that he's probably met lots of Royalty before. But I didn't really know. He didn't talk much about his childhood or life before coming to America to work at Ashworth and Kent.

"What's tomorrow, Master?"

"We are having a special event at the club for a visiting foreign dignitary."

Something told me there was more to this event than Devlin was letting on but as Mistress Sophie and I discussed earlier, I need to learn to trust Devlin in all aspects of my life. So if he wanted me to know he would tell me.

"Is he a real Prince?"

"Yes, from some country in the Middle East. I'm not sure which one."

"I'm so excited. Is there anything special I should wear?"

"You can wear anything you want my slave," Devlin said as he kissed me.

Mistress Sophie stood up and said her goodbyes before snapping her fingers and calling for her slave to be by her side. She attached his leash and they headed out the door.

When they were gone Devlin turned his attention back to me.

"Did you and Mistress Sophie have fun tonight?"

I giggled. "We did."

Chapter 17

I was excited all day about meeting a real Prince.
I couldn't wait until it was time to go. Devlin took me to
get my hair and makeup done at the salon and even let
me pick which dress I wanted to wear. He decided on
my shoes but that's okay, he had great taste and the
black super high pumps he picked matched the dress I
selected perfectly. It was a very short and fitted that
clung to my every curve. The dress itself wasn't anything
special, but what made it unique was the long sheer
chiffon sleeves. It added an extra layer of sophistication
to an otherwise normal boring black dress.

"Do you think I can wear my Swarovski crystal
slave necklace tonight Master?"

"Of course you can my sweet. I told you, tonight
you can wear anything you want."

"Thank you Master."

He got out the gemstone studded necklace that
spelled out slave in beautiful shiny Swarovski crystals
and put it around my neck.

It wasn't until we were on our way to the club
that Devlin told me about the auction that was going to
take place.

"How does that work Master? Where do the
slaves come from?"

It depends on the type of auction. If it's for a weekend or short period of time then usually it's another Master putting up his slave. He is auctioning off the use of the slave but when the agreed upon time is over the slave returns to his or her original Master."

"So you could sell me off to another Master for the day?"

"I could if so inclined."

"Is that the kind of auction going on tonight?"

"No, tonight's auction is for permanent ownership. A person auctions themselves off to be someone's slave. "

"Why would someone agree to auction themselves off to someone they don't know to be their slave?"

"There are a lot of reasons. Some do it for the money, some do it to meet different Dom's, allowing them to experience different philosophies and techniques of training."

"How much does a slave go for at auction?"

"Like anything up for sale, it really depends on the quality of the goods. I've never seen a slave at a club auction go for more than $100,000 but I suppose with the right girl it could happen."

Devlin playfully patted my thigh and a chill ran down my spine.

"How many girls will be auctioned off tonight Master?"

"There will only be three slaves up for auction tonight but that isn't the big draw. After the slaves are auctioned off there will be a special guest."

"The Prince?"

Devlin chuckled. "No. Tonight they will be auctioning off a girls virginity."

I turned my head to look at Devlin. Surely I heard him wrong. There was no way this could be real.

Devlin smiled and rubbed my leg assuredly. "Don't worry she's an adult. The girl turned eighteen about a month ago."

"Okay so she's old enough to vote, buy cigarettes and join the military. That doesn't really make it any better. It's her virginity, that isn't something she can ever get back."

We pulled into the parking lot of the club and Devlin got out of the car to open my door. Before going in though he boxed me in, with my back to the car.

"The girls who do this volunteer. They'll make more money tonight than most people will in their entire lives."

I couldn't believe he was justifying this with money. "A young girl's virginity isn't a commodity to be bought and sold."

"You had the right to do whatever you wanted with your body and your virginity but now you want to tell this girl and others like her what they can and can't do with their own. Selling your virginity may not be something you would ever do, but we shouldn't be so quick to judge others."

I leaned in and kissed Devlin. "You are right Master. I never really thought about it like that before."

Devlin snapped on my leash and we walked into the club.

I don't know what I was expecting when it came to the Prince but I most definitely wasn't expecting him to be so good looking. He looked so normal. If it weren't for all the security around him, I don't think I would have even known he was royalty. He had shaggy brown hair and big soulful brown eyes that dominated his face. When he looked at you, he just seemed to emanate warmth and strength.

He had so many people around him, we never got the chance to actually talk to him. But throughout the night I swore it felt like he was watching me. It was probably just my imagination though so I tried to put the thought out of my mind.

Soon they brought the slaves out who would be auctioned off. There would be fifteen minutes for anyone interested in bidding to examine the merchandise.

The girls were for the most part pretty. They all looked to be in their early twenties and they all had light brown hair. From a distance they could probably be mistaken for sisters.

When the bidding began everyone was taken into the theater room and took their seats, as if we were going to watch a movie, only this was real, very real, and when it was all said and done someone was going to buy another human being and she would have to submit to his every whim.

I think what scared me most about the whole thing is knowing that Devlin could very well auction me off at any time if he grew tired of me and there was really nothing I could do about it.

I tried to push those thoughts out of my mind as the girls were brought on stage and the first one was placed front and center. The bidding began at $25,000. It started off slow but in the end she went for $52,000. The second girl was auctioned off for $49,000 and the final girl, who was by far the prettiest of the three, went for $64,000.

As I watched the girls being carted off backstage, I wondered how much of that money they got to keep and what in the world they needed that kind of money for in the first place. They were all so young, so they couldn't possibly have much debt. Maybe they were going to use the money to pay for college or to help buy a house. I guess what they wanted the money for really didn't matter, but it was still all I could think about when I saw them being taken away in chains.

Next they brought up the young virgin and an older gentleman dressed in a fancy tuxedo told a little about her. She was originally from Brazil and moved to the United States to live with her aunt and uncle when her parents died a few years ago. Although her native language is Portuguese she speaks fluent English. She turned eighteen last month and she has several documents to prove she is of the legal age of consent. Her virginity had been medically certified and she has not left the watchful eye of her caretakers since that certification has taken place. After going over specifics of the medical certification of her virginity they began to talk about her measurements.

"This young girl stands five foot four inches tall and weighs one hundred and eleven pounds. Her measurements are 32B-26-34. She has no tattoos or visible scars," the man said.

She looked so sweet and vulnerable with her big doe eyes. I just couldn't help but feel sorry for her. Did she know what she was getting into? Was this her idea or did someone else put her up to it? Even if it was her idea, how in the world did she find these people to help her make it happen? I wondered if this was something Devlin's club did all the time, or did they just auction off young virgins when they had special visitors like the Prince come to town? Where they auctioning off virgins in every location of the club all around the world, or did they just do that in the Houston location?

The bidding began at $150,000 and quickly rose to $1.2 million. I was shocked that someone would be willing to spend more than a million dollars for a single night with this girl. She was cute, really adorable, but I can't say I would spend a million dollars to have sex with her. Then again, I can't say that I would ever spend a million dollars to have sex with anyone, even Angelina Jolie or Kate Upton. Not even for both of them at the same time. That's just crazy.

I noticed that the Prince was watching the young girl with great interest but he hadn't bid yet. After a few more bids from others, he lifted his paddle and said "three million dollars."

There was a lot of hushed chatter and with that, the young virgin was his. His security team gathered up the girl and took her away. I wasn't sure where she went but I noticed the Prince stayed around which surprised me, I would have thought he would have wanted to rush off and claim his prize. I mean how often can you really say you get to spend the night with a certified virgin? He didn't even seem that excited about his prize.

With the auction now complete, everyone started making their way out of the theatre and back to the grand ballroom. While Devlin was leading me out I turned my head to look at the Prince who was surrounded by people congratulating him on his purchase. But while they were looking at him, he was looking at me. Our eyes locked and I knew then I wasn't crazy, he had been watching me. It wasn't all just in my imagination.

When we got back into the grand ballroom we made our way over to the bar for a drink. Devlin suggested this time I try the pomegranate champagne which was really just pomegranate juice mixed in with expensive champagne. It was good and I had just taken a sip when I saw a familiar face smiling back at me. Mistress Sophie ran up to me and gave me a hug hello.

"Did you just get here? I've been looking for you," I asked her.

"No my baby girl, I've been here all night. I've just been busy chatting with the Prince. Have you had the chance to meet him yet?"

"No he's had so many people around him all night. Wait, you know the Prince?"

"Sort of, our families know each other through business. Would you like an introduction?"

I turned to Devlin. "May we go meet him Master?"

"Sure," he answered reluctantly. I held his hand and Mistress Sophie led us over through the small crowd that surrounded the Prince.

"Your Highness, this is my good friend Master D," Mistress Sophie said to the Prince.

The Prince politely shook Devlin's hand and then turned to me. "And who might this lovely lady be?"

"This is my Mary Elizabeth," Devlin replied.

When I held my hand out to shake his, the Prince grabbed my hand and kissed it instead. "The beautiful Mary Elizabeth."

I don't know what came over me, but I suddenly felt playful.

"Amy, my name is Amy," I corrected.

The Prince stepped back and just looked at me. Everyone around him just gasped. Apparently correcting the Prince when he makes a mistake isn't allowed.

He started to apologize and I giggled. I stepped up, closing the distance between us and playfully put my hand on his arm. "I'm only teasing. My name is really Mary Elizabeth."

The Prince looked at me in confusion.

"Everyone seemed to be so serious around you, I just thought you needed a laugh."

Those who stood around him were notably quiet, all seeming to hold their breath, wondering what the Prince would do next. When he let out a big belly laugh, everyone relaxed.

"Miss Mary Elizabeth, I like you. Most people who meet me shy away from being themselves. They are afraid to do or say anything that thing think might offend me. You are a credit to your Master."

I curtseyed. "Thank you, Your Highness. I don't know what came over me. It's just everyone was standing around being so serious, I just wanted to make you smile."

The Prince turned to Devlin. "Have you had a chance to see the Salvador Dali?"

"No, not yet. Mary Elizabeth and I were headed up there when we ran into Mistress Sophie."

Devlin and the Prince made small talk for a few more minutes before we parted ways and made our way up the marble stairs to see this thing they were talking about.

"Master, who or what is this Salvador Dali thing you and the Prince were talking about?"

"One of the members donated a $150,000 Salvador Dali painting."

"Is he a member of your club?"

Devlin chuckled. "No my slave, Salvador Dali is a famous surrealist painter. He died years ago."

"What does that mean Master?"

"Surrealism means beyond real or logical. You take real subjects and present them in a dreamlike way."

I guess that kind of made sense. I didn't really understand what it meant, but we had finally arrived at the painting and I got distracted by looking at it and trying to figure out what in the world made someone think the painting was worth $150,000. I most definitely am not a fine art connoisseur.

Out of the corner of my eye I noticed Mistress Sophie standing near the railing, looking over the balcony. I grabbed a new champagne as the waiter walked by and went to talk to her, leaving Devlin to speak to his friends about the merits of supporting the arts.

"What is that lovely fragrance you have on? That's new right?" Mistress Sophie asked me.

"Master got it for me last week. It's Flora by Gucci."

"He does love spoiling you."

I giggled. "Yes, he does. I'm very lucky to have him."

I leaned over the railing to see what was down there. I noticed the Prince standing next to a large stone statue. It was big, much taller than him. From my height, I couldn't tell what the statue was of, but the Prince looked rather interested in it. That was until he glanced up and seen me looking down at him.

I blushed, embarrassed that he caught me staring, but I didn't look away. That was until I noticed his eyes grow larger, as if he was seeing something going on behind me. I heard a loud crunch and when I turned my head wondering what caused that horrified look on his face I seen Mistress Sophie reaching out for me, while at the same time her slave was holding her back.

The next thing I remember is being in the Prince's arms and him smiling down at me and then nothing -- complete and utter blackness.

Chapter 18

When I finally came to I was in the hospital and my beloved Devlin was sitting in a chair next to my bed, holding my hand.

I opened my eyes and slowly took in my surroundings. On one side of the room was a bunch of machines that I found myself attached to. On the other side was Devlin and at the foot of my bed was Mistress Sophie pacing back and forth while her slave stood in the corner diligently, always by her side.

I squeezed Devlin's hand just about the same time Mistress Sophie realized I was coming to. Devlin jumped out of his chair and told her to go get the nurse and let her know I was awake.

"Master, what happened?"

He learned down and kissed my forehead.

"There was an accident, my sweet. You are in the hospital. Do you remember any of it?"

Devlin helped me sit up in my bed and my hand immediately went to the bump on my forehead. It was throbbing. I thought about the party we had been at and tried to remember what happened.

"I don't know. I remember talking to Mistress Sophie. She liked my Gucci perfume."

As Mistress Sophie walked back into the room I remembered seeing her face as I was falling and her slave holding on to her to keep her from falling too. Soon after Mistress Sophie returned the doctor came in to check on me. Mistress Sophie and her slave went outside while the doctor was with me but Devlin stayed.

The doctor examined me thoroughly. He read over my chart and then gave us the good news.

"Looks like you had a nasty little fall but all of your tests came back clean."

He flipped through a few more pages on his chart. "No concussion, that's good. That bump on your head will no doubt cause you some pain over the next few days but we'll give you something for that. It will probably make you tired so no driving or operating heavy machinery.

"As far as the other injuries go, you might want to consider increasing your vitamin C intake, maybe drink an extra glass of orange juice each morning with your breakfast. It will help the contusions heal quicker."

I blushed when I realized he was talking about the red markings on my butt from where Devlin had been spanking me.

"You may also want to try eating more leafy vegetables."

I giggled. "Okay thank you doctor. I will."

The doctor continued reading my chart and making notes. "Doctor, when do you think I'll be able to go home?"

"I just signed your release. I'll hand it over to the nurses after this. They will take some time to get all of your discharge papers but you'll be free to go then."

When the doctor left the room Mistress Sophie and her slave came back in.

"How long was I out Master?"

"Not long. They gave you something when we arrived, so they could run their tests on your head and that may have been part of the reason you were out so long."

"How do you feel?" Mistress Sophie asked.

"Tired. Confused. I don't know. I still can't believe all of this. How did I fall?"

Mistress Sophie looked to Devlin who nodded his head as if he was telling her it was okay to give me the story.

"Someone behind us tripped and fell over, landing on the railing that you were leaning on. When it broke he fell and so did you. The Prince was in the right place at the right time and caught you."

"I can't believe it. How about the other guy, is he okay?"

"I think I heard he had a broken arm or leg or something. He'll be fine though."

Before we could finish our conversation there was a knock on the door and then a policeman came into my room.

"May we help you with something officer?" Devlin asked.

"I just need to get a statement from Miss Seabrook."

"Please, call me Elizabeth."

"Okay Miss Elizabeth, why don't you tell me what you remember about your fall?"

I looked to Devlin, nervous to speak openly with the police officer. Devlin smiled down at me and nodded his head as if it were okay to speak, so I did.

"I don't know what you mean. How far back should I go?"

"Well, let's start with the beginning. What was the event you were attending tonight?"

"My boyfriend Devlin and I went to a party. It was a social gathering to honor the Prince's visit."

"Do you know what he was doing here in Texas?"

"No I don't know. I'm sorry." I looked to Devlin to see if he could answer. "Devlin do you know?"

The officer however interrupted before he could answer.

"Don't worry Miss Seabrook. We have everyone else's statements already. I just want to see what you know and how things went from your point of view. It's okay if you are aren't sure."

"Then no, I'm sorry but I don't know why he is here. I just assumed some oil business or something."

"Was this the first time you've ever met the Prince?"

"Yes. Prior to meeting him tonight, I didn't know who he was. I don't even know what country he's a Prince of. All I know is that it's somewhere in the Middle East."

"And when you were at this social gathering, what did you do? Please take me through what you remember. Try and specifically think of anyone you might have seen or anything that stands out in your mind."

"When we first came in I noticed a lady wearing a long red dress. I recognized it immediately from the Prada contour collection. I was on their website last week and seen it up there. It was bright red but because the fabric was so sheer it made it look more faded, you know what I mean?"

"I don't, but that's okay. Think carefully about the other people at the party. Did anyone else stand out to you?"

I thought about it for a moment.

"Just say the first thing that comes to mind."

"Oh yes, there was something that stood out to me. Before we went up the stairs we went over to the table where they were serving drinks and there was this girl standing there in metallic Jimmy Choo's. They were so amazing"

Mistress Sophie chimed in. "I seen those. I know exactly who you mean."

The police officer just sighed.

"Did anything else stick out to you during the course of the night that perhaps wasn't fashion related?"

"I'm sorry. I could tell you that two different ladies had the exact same Chanel dress on but in different colors and styled with different accessories but still, I knew it was the same dress. I could tell you that someone there, a really tall blonde lady had on a dress from the Marc Jacob collection from a year or so ago. It was from the show that Kendall Jenner walked the runway with no eyebrows. But if you want to know something other than what people wore that night, I just don't know if I can be of much help."

"Did you see the man who fell onto the railing?"

"No. I was looking down at this stone statue when he fell. I didn't seem him before or after."

"Was this the statue that fell on the Prince and put him in the coma?"

"What? What do you mean? The Prince is in a coma?"

I looked to Devlin for an explanation and then back to the police officer.

"I'm sorry ma'am I didn't realize you didn't know."

Devlin rubbed my arm soothingly. "It's okay Mary Elizabeth. We'll talk about it later. Please continue officer, the nurse will be back soon with her discharge papers and we want to get her out of here and back home."

"Okay, Miss Seabrook, I mean Elizabeth," the office corrected himself. "Did you have any personal interaction with the Prince during the party?"

"Devlin and I spoke to him briefly. He was always surrounded by so many people. As I'm sure you can imagine, everyone wanted a minute of his time. I mean how often do you get to meet a real life Prince?"

"What did you speak about?"

"It was nothing really. We said hello and then he talked to Devlin about some fancy painting and then that was really it."

"And you are sure nothing during the entire night stuck out in your mind as unusual or out of place?"

"There was a lady with his group almost the entire time. She had on this crazy looking Emilio Pucci dress."

"What was so crazy about her dress?"

"Oh well it wasn't the dress per say. It was ... well, Emilio Pucci is known for these insane patterns. Her dress was white and had the crazy patterns but it wasn't colorful like normal, the patterns were outlined in silver and the sleeves had this cool fringe. I don't know. I guess it stuck out in my mind because normally he has such bold prints and this dress was so classy. Not that his stuff isn't normally classy. I don't know, it's hard to explain. I wouldn't have even known it was by Emilio Pucci if I hadn't overheard someone else mention it."

He let out an exasperated sigh. "Okay, Miss Seabrook. That's very nice, but I meant anything that wasn't fashion related."

"Well …. No. Fashion is what sticks out to me. If someone is in a great dress or some fabulous shoes, that I'm going to notice. But put a man with a gun next to someone's head and I probably wouldn't even have realized it. I'm sorry. I know that's not what you want to hear but it's the truth. I can't help it. I'm a girl so I notice girly things."

The officer was clearly annoyed but continued with his line of questioning.

"According to several eye witness accounts, when the Prince caught you in his arms he appears to have lost his footing. He began to fall backwards, which is when you banged your head on the stone statue. You both fell to the ground and he covered you with his body to protect you from further harm and that's when the statue came down on him, knocking him out. Is that how you would describe the events as well?"

"I don't know. I'm sorry. I don't remember what happened. I don't remember falling at all. I remember landing in the Prince's arms and him smiling down at me and that's it. The next thing I remember is waking up here in the hospital. The doctor said I may remember little things in the next day or two but other than that I can't help you."

The police officer handed his card to me and after glancing down at it, I gave it to Devlin.

"Okay Miss Seabrook, thank you for your time. If you happen to remember anything that you think might be of importance please call the number on my card."

Mistress Sophie showed the officer out of the room while Devlin fluffed my pillow to make me more comfortable.

When she returned she had a huge smile on her face, trying her best to hold back a laugh.

"Okay Miss thing, when did you become such a fashion expert?"

I grinned, knowing I was completely busted.

"What gave me away?"

"You and I both know there was nobody there in a red Prada dress."

I giggled.

"I admit, when the police showed up and started speaking with you before your Master and I had a

237

chance to go over some things with you, I was a little nervous but you my dear were amazing. I couldn't have been more impressed. Where in the world did you come up with such a great misdirection like that?"

"When I worked at Ashworth and Kent we had a client who had to come in because her parents were making some adjustments to her trust. Their family wealth had increased considerably so they were going to put more money into her trust. Instead of being grateful or helpful in any way she just sat there going on and on about fashion and Prada this and Donna Karen that. Everyone was so annoyed with her. She was absolutely the worst client I ever had to deal with. I just channeled her and that way I could answer and seem helpful without actually saying anything useful."

Devlin leaned down and kissed my forehead. "You are brilliant my sweet."

"What do you think is taking so long with my discharge Master? Do you think something is wrong?"

"No of course not. They are probably just busy. I'll go to the nurse's station and see what I can find while Mistress Sophie helps you get dressed."

I jumped out of bed and hurried to get dressed while Devlin went to find one of the nurses.

"Okay let's go," I said to a stunned Mistress Sophie.

"What do you mean baby girl?"

"I need you to help me to go see the Prince. I need to see him. I need to know that he's okay."

"There is no way we can get in to see him, he's in intensive care. They only let immediate family in to see patients in that ward."

"Then you can help me sneak in. Please Mistress Sophie. I can't do it without you."

She sighed. "Fine. But if we get caught it's all on you."

We quickly but discreetly made our way over to the ICU and found the Prince's two guards distracted by flirting with the nurses. Mistress Sophie went up to speak to them, while her slave's big body blocked their view and I snuck into the room behind him.

Once inside I found the Prince hooked up to all kinds of machinery. I held his hand and began to cry. I couldn't believe he was in a coma and it was all my fault. He was like this because he tried to save me.

As I was telling him that I wanted him to get better I felt him squeeze my hand. And right about that time a member of his security team came in and found me.

"Hey you there. What are you doing in here? Get away from him."

His other guard came in next and then some of the hospital staff. As they were pulling me away I shouted for them to stop.

"Please wait. He squeezed my hand. He's awake."

There was so much madness and chaos with all the hospital staff running around checking out the machines and his vitals and with his security trying to force me out of the room, they just wouldn't listen to me.

Devlin found me and dragged me back to my own room with Mistress Sophie and her slave following close behind. I could tell by the look on his face and the strong grip he had on my arm that Devlin was not happy with me.

"What the hell do you think you were doing?"

"I'm sorry Master. I just wanted to make sure the Prince was okay."

"You could have caused a serious international incident. Do you not realize this? He's not just any normal person. He's a Prince. Do you not understand what that means?"

"You are right, I'm sorry. I just wanted to make sure he was okay."

I began to sob uncontrollably but Devlin wasn't moved. He was still very angry that I snuck into see the Prince.

"Sophie, damn it. You know how volatile things are with his people. What were you thinking?"

"I couldn't stop her. She had her little mind set on going to see the Prince. What was I supposed to do sit on her and hold her down until you returned?"

Devlin just rolled his eyes. Mistress Sophie may have denied any involvement in my little stunt but Devlin wasn't stupid, he knew better.

"Well if the three of you are finished causing trouble we can get out of here now. I have her discharge papers."

I didn't see Mistress Sophie for the next few days but then again, I didn't see much of anything in that time. Whatever medicine the doctors prescribed, made me sleep and sleep and sleep.

When I did finally come to, I made my way to the living room to find Devlin putting another package on the coffee table.

"What are all of these boxes Master?"

It seems that Mistress Sophie has been busy.

"These are all from her?"

"No. I meant that she has been busy telling some of the other members of the club about your police report. They thought it rather amusing and wanted to send you a gift to show their appreciation for your discretion in dealing with the authorities."

"So all of these gifts are for me, from your friends at the club?"

"It seems so. Feel up to opening them?"

"Oh, Master. I can't believe it. There are so many of them."

I sat on the floor next to the coffee table and began opening the packages. There were at least forty of them in all and each box had some expensive designer outfit.

There were dresses from Prada, Ralph Lauren, Gucci, Armani, Burberry, and Zac Posen. Some of the gifts were shoes, all beautiful high heels of various colors from different designers. Some I had never even heard of like Salvatore Ferragamo and Stuart Weitzman. Everything was so elegant and clearly expensive. I felt bad that his friends were lavishing me with so many nice things when I didn't really do anything.

"Master do you think we could go to Hallmark to buy some blank thank you cards? I would like to hand write some notes of gratitude to everyone who sent me a gift."

"I think I have some in my office. I'll dig them out for you later."

There was one last box for me to open. It was so small I almost missed it in the pile of others. Inside there was a note that said, "A rare gem for a rare gem". The card was not signed.

The gift was a breathtakingly beautiful, gold and black diamond bracelet. I had never seen anything like it. Devlin helped me put it on my wrist and then we gathered up all the other gifts and brought them to my bedroom so I could put them away.

Chapter 19

Devlin went to find the thank you cards, while I put everything away. I gathered up all the cards so that I could use them for the thank you notes I would be writing up. I noticed several of them made mention of how they looked forward to my presentation.

"Master, what is this presentation everyone is talking about?"

"I was going to wait until you felt better to discuss it, but I suppose now will do."

Devlin sat down next to me on the bed. I didn't know what it was he was about to say to me but I could tell by the look on his face that I wasn't going to like it.

"The presentation is a ritual that dates back to ancient Roman times. Back then when a Master fell in love with his slave they had to be sure that the slave truly loved his Master and would be willing to do anything for him. They wanted to make sure that the slave wasn't just saying that they did, for money. It's easy to say you love someone, but they wanted to make sure that the love was true and that the slave would in fact be willing to do anything for their Master which would prove their love was genuine."

What Devlin said made sense. But still I knew there had to be something more to this. I desperately feared for what he wasn't saying.

"So for us to be together forever, you must be presented to the members of the club. The ritual will take place once you are fully recovered from the fall."

"What happens during this ritual Master?"

Devlin pulled me into his arms and held me tightly. "Don't be scared my slave. If you truly love me then you will be able to make it through the ritual."

I did love Devlin but would I really put myself through some ancient pagan based ritual that probably included lots of pain and torture from countless people? Did I even have a choice?

"What would I wear?"

"You don't wear anything."

"What? I'm to be presented to these people completely naked?"

He continued to hold me tightly but it wasn't helping to calm me as it normally did. I pulled away from him so I could see his face.

"I don't think I can do this. I just don't."

"You don't think you can or you don't want to?"

"I don't want to stand in front of all of those people naked. The initiation was hard on me. I had nightmares about it for weeks after."

"The initiation and presentation aren't the same. The initiation is something all the Masters do for fun. It's not organization or structured. The presentation is more ritualistic and dates back to ancient Roman times."

"Will I be naked in front of people I don't know?"

"Yes."

"Will these strangers be spanking me?"

"Yes."

"Then to me it's exactly like the initiation. I don't see a difference."

I expected Devlin to be angry with me, but surprisingly he wasn't. He remained calm the entire time.

"It's sort of like the difference between going to your high school prom and having a wedding. While it's true they both have similarities, they aren't exactly the same and in the end, if you miss your high school prom it's no big deal but if you don't have a wedding, then you miss out on an important part of the bonding process between you and another person, the person that supposed to mean the world to you."

Devlin put his hand on my chin, forcing me to look up at him.

"I love you Mary Elizabeth and I want to spend the rest of my life with you. I thought you felt the same way about me. But if you don't feel like you are ready to make that kind of commitment to me, then I need to know now."

I started to cry. Was this his way of saying he wanted to marry me? Or is this just some sort of ritualistic beating. It's all just so overwhelming. I didn't know what to do or think or say.

"I want to be with someone who wants to be with me. I thought that's what I had with you, but clearly I was mistaken."

As I sat there crying I remembered my talk with Mistress Sophie. It was then I knew this was not a test for my love of Devlin. Obviously I loved him. It didn't matter what those people said or thought. I knew that I loved him. The test was of my ability to let go. I needed to fully trust Devlin if we were going to spend the rest of our lives together.

It is easy to say I love you, but to mean it you have to let go. You have to trust that the other person truly will take care of you and have that blind faith in them. I keep saying that I trust Devlin but at the first chance to prove it, I back away. I know now that I have to go through with this presentation. I have to let go of my fears and trust in Devlin. I have to trust in our love and know that no matter what, he will always be there for me.

"You are right. I have to believe in you and us. I will walk on broken glass or put hot coals on my body if that's what I have to do to prove my devotion to your friends at the club."

Devlin pulled me up off of the bed and held me tightly in his arms again.

"What made you change your mind?"

"Because I don't ever want you to question my love for you Devlin. If this is what it takes to make you see that I truly love you with all of my heart, then that is what I will do. I love you and I will spend the rest of my life showing you just how much."

He leaned in to kiss me and then ran his hands slowly over my breasts. My hands fell to my side and he trailed kisses along my neck. I let out a gasp as his hand found its way between my legs. He was running his fingers between my legs, searching, exploring.

As he continued, I let out a soft moan, reached down and grabbed his shaft. His hardness tightened again my fingers.

He pushed my hands away. "Not yet."

Leaning down he ran tiny kisses along my jawline, then down my arm to the tip of my middle finger. His touch was unusually gentle. He moved slowly, his strokes were like loving caresses.

I laid down and wrapped my legs around his back as he slid deep inside of me. I was willing and wet and thrust my hips upwards, wanting more of him.

"You feel incredible inside of me," I breathed. "I could stay like this forever."

He smiled and began to slowly roll his hips. Soon he picked up speed, jarring my body with each stroke. I cried out as I felt my grip on reality slipping. I could feel pleasure rising up to take me away. I moaned and held on to him tightly and my climax took over me. My fingernails digging into his chest.

I held on to him tightly and then felt his cock jerk hard inside of me, following by the warm spray of his seed.

After, I closed my eyes and locked my legs around his waist, wanting to keep him inside me forever.

His body relaxed on top of me. His weight felt safe and comforting as it pressed me into the bed. We laid like that for several minutes without speaking.

I let me nails lightly trail down his spine and then I kissed him passionately.

"Is this your way of saying you are ready to go for another round my sweet?"

I giggled. "Oh goodness no. I'm worn out."

Devlin rolled off of my and held me tightly in his arms as I fell asleep.

Chapter 20

I may have committed to going through with the presentation but I was scared to death. I had no idea what they were going to do to me however if the initiation was any indication, I was most assuredly going to be beaten and bruised from head to toe and it's hard to psych yourself up for that.

The day before the ritual I was taken away. I wasn't allowed to have any contact with Devlin a full twenty four hours beforehand. Luckily I had Mistress Sophie who was by my side the entire time. I don't know where her slave was but she stayed the night with me in the special room they had set up for me at the club.

The next morning we enjoyed a long and soothing body massage and then relaxed in the steam room. After lunch Mistress Sophie had some things to take care of so I decided to take a nap.

When I woke up several females from the club gave me what they called a ceremonial bath. I was taken to a room with glass walls and in the middle there was a round pool. It was filled with special water taken from the source of the Tiber River in Rome, two natural springs on Mount Fumaiolo. In the pool hundreds and hundreds of rose petals floated all about.

As the woman helped me into the pool, one of the ladies explained what was going on. They walked me down the steps and stopped when the water came up to just past my waist. They laid me on my back and I was floating on the water with all of the women surrounding me, helping me to stay afloat.

"The purpose of the ritual bath is to cleanse you, both inside and out. We want to cleanse your body, mind and soul of impurities and negative energies. Relax and enjoy the warmth of the water, the scent in the air and the feeling of being purified."

Blessed be your mind so that you may understand your Master's wisdom.

Blessed be your eyes so that you may see the love your Master has for you.

Blessed be your heart, so that your love for your Master is pure and kind.

Blessed be your hands that have touched your Master.

Blessed be your feet that have taken you to your Master.

Blessed be your lips, as they have kept your Masters secrets.

They walked me out of the pool and as we stood on the last step the main lady spoke up again.

"From this moment on you have been cleansed of your past deeds. You are free from your previous mistakes. You will step forward not letting your past guide your actions or choices. Let love touch you, and set your heart free."

It's strange really how something as simple as a bath or a swim in a pool can be so dramatic and life changing. But being here now with all of these ladies, I really do feel different.

I was taken from the pool back to my bedroom and told to wait, that someone would come to gather me soon.

A doctor came into my room and gave me a thorough examination. She said I had to be certified medically fit before they could proceed. She check my body for open sores and gave me a vaginal exam as well, to ensure I wasn't with child.

Just as she finished up with me Mistress Sophie returned to help me get dressed. I was to wear a flowing gown that was sheer and really did nothing to actually cover my body. I felt completely naked in the dress. You could see everything. To make matters worse, I was not allowed to wear panties or a bra, so I felt even more exposed.

Mistress Sophie stayed with me until the men came to get me. There were three of them and they were all bald and wore nothing but a white loincloth. They didn't speak to me at all as they escorted downstairs to the basement of the building and down a long dimly lit hallway. My first thought was that I was going to be taken to a dingy dungeon and beaten half to death.

But as we arrived at our destination I found that wasn't the case at all. The room was huge, and well decorated. It looked like it might have been a royal throne room in a medieval castle. In the middle of the large room was a raised circle that looked to be made of marble and in the middle of that was a wheel of death, like you would see a knife thrower use.

The second I laid eyes on that wheel I knew I was in trouble. I took a step back, but there was nowhere to run. The three totally shaven men in loincloths nudged me forward to the center circle and then removed my gown. I stood there, frozen in place, too scared to move a single muscle or say a word.

As they slipped the dress off I realized for the first time we weren't alone in the room. A hundred men, maybe more stood in the dimly lit archways staring at the men removing my clothes.

A large man wearing a black hooded cloak stepped onto the platform.

"Step forward my child."

His voice was loud and deep and scared the shit out of me when he spoke, but I did as I was told and took a step closer to him.

"Today we have the presentation of Master D's slave, Mary Elizabeth. Those who wish to participate, please step forward."

As the man said that, about thirty men and women stepped forward, each of them also wore long, black hooded cloaks. They were all squeezed together in a circle, and I knew these were going to be the men and women that were going to beat me. All I could do now was hope and pray that it wouldn't be as bad as what the initiation was.

"In my hand I hold a jar of freshly pressed oil that has been made from olives that come from a branch that has been preserved from tree's that were grown by Augustus Caesar himself."

The three bald men picked me up, holding my body length wise, like I was a plank of wood. The master of ceremonies then poured the oil on me and the first hooded member of the crowd stepped forward to rub it in. The oil continued to be poured on my body as one by one every hooded person standing in the circle had their chanced to rub it into my body. Some focused on my stomach, while others rubbed it into my breasts and others my thighs. Half way through I was turned over and my backside was covered and rubbed. By the time it was over there wasn't a single inch of my body that wasn't thoroughly covered in the olive oil.

Next the three bald men took me over to the wheel of death, securing my wrists and ankles in the attached cuffs.

The three bald men started chanting, "Amor est vitae essentia. Amor Vincit Omnia." I don't know what it meant, but I tried to focus on their words to help push back the fear.

Then one by one each person came and hit me with a flogger three times, while chanting "ut amore et ostenditis". As they hit me the wheel would begin to spin. When the person was finished and began to walk away, the three bald chanting men stopped it from spinning and I had just enough time to regain my wits before the next person came up to do it all over again. This went on until all thirty of the men and women had their turn with me. The pain was excruciating. There was no part of my body that didn't scream out in agony.

When Devlin first told me about the presentation I couldn't understand how going through some ritual could prove your love to your Master. But now I totally get it. Any slave willing to put themselves through this kind of pain and suffering for their Master in front of people no less, must truly love him.

When the last person was finished hitting me with their flogger three times, the three bald men removed me from the wheel of death and held me in their arms as the master of ceremonies again poured the oil on my body, front and back.

The wheel of death was removed from the platform and in its place was a round bed. I began to panic, worried they might expect me to have sex with one or maybe all of the people here. I didn't know what was going to happen but as the three bald men laid me on the bed, I seen Devlin's smiling face standing over me.

Then it hit me, these people expected me to make love to Devlin right here on this bed, in front of everyone.

After all the beatings and the rub downs and the chanting and medical exams and purifications, I wasn't sure if this was something I could do. It was just too much. It was over the line. I couldn't do this.

Devlin crouched between my legs and as I looked in his eyes, all my nervousness and apprehension went away. Suddenly it was just the two of us and the rest of the world didn't matter.

He brushed his fingers across the outer lips of my pussy and the sensation caused a shiver to run up my spine.

I spread my legs slightly and that was all the encouragement he needed. He bent down and began licking my pussy. He pushed at my legs, forcing me to spread them wider. He ran his thumb gently against my clit and then inserted a finger inside of me and then another.

The pressure was building and I knew if he continued to stroke me like that, I was going to explode soon.

When he began flicking his tongue in and out of me, I grabbed his hair and started running my fingers through it. I started to whimper and buck against his mouth.

I desperately wanted to come and I knew I was close. That was until I heard the chanting. The three bald men had returned, standing near the head softly repeating their strange and mesmerizing words.

Devlin stopped what he was doing, grabbing me by the back of my head, and rammed his tongue inside of my mouth, forcing me to taste my own juices. I hungrily kissed him back.

He pulled my head back, so he could look at my face. Before I knew what was happening he spun me around, grabbing me by the waist and pushed my face into the bed, forcing my ass in the air.

He held on to my hips as he rammed his cock inside of me. I cried out with both pleasure and pain. I could hear the men still chanting as Devlin slammed his cock in and out of me.

I arched my back as Devlin continued to thrust deep inside of me. Our bodies bucked and rocked against each other rhythmically.

I felt his balls smacking against my pussy as he slammed his cock in and out of me. Then he pulled halfway back and shoved all the way in again, holding it deep inside me for a few moments.

He hastened his pace, pulling his long shaft nearly all the way out before plunging it all the way back in. I've never felt so completely filled before.

I could feel my orgasm building up inside of me as he moved his cock inside of me. Finally it was just too much for my body to handle. With each deep thrust, he hit the spot, stoking the fire inside of me.

He was fast and furious, fucking me mercilessly. I grabbed the sheets and buried my face into the mattress, hoping to muffle my screams as I reached the edge.

My body tensed up and he knew I was coming. I could never hide that from him and he slowed down for just a moment while the waves of pleasure washed over me.

Devlin wasn't finished with me yet though. He started to pull out and then before I knew it, he thrust himself deep inside of me. Just as he started working up another steady pace, I felt a sharp sting across my back.

One of the hooded men who stood around us in a circle had now stepped forward and began hitting me with his flogger. I cried out in pain but Devlin didn't stop fucking me.

The others soon took their turns and eventually the pain transformed to into a satisfying feeling of fulfillment. It was a strange sensation that I've never known before. In my mind I could no longer make out the difference between the pleasure of Devlin fucking me and the pain of being flogged.

Soon I could feel Devlin's cock throbbing inside of me, in the way that it did before he was about to come. His body tensed up in preparation for the explosion that was to come. Then I felt it, his cock swelled and exploded inside of me. His body shuddered as he released himself fully.

The flogging stopped and he collapsed onto the bed next to me. I tried to just relax and breath, hoping it would make the pain easier to bear.

It didn't. I hurt all over. I didn't know what was going to happen next. I just wanted it to be over so I could go home and cry. I didn't want these people to see me cry.

The three bald men picked me up off of the bed and carried me back down the long dimly lit hall and to my room.

The sat me carefully onto my bed. I hurt too much to move so I laid there until Devlin came for me. I was too weak to try and move on my own so Devlin dressed me and carried me to the car. That was the last thing I remembered before falling asleep. When I came to Devlin and I were back home alone and the whole nightmare of the presentation was over.

Thanks to a cocktail of sleeping pills and pain killers, I slept away the next few days while my body recovered.

When I wasn't sleeping Devlin was taking care of my every need. He even laid in bed with me and read stories to me from my favorite romance novels. Listening to his soothing voice as he read to me was the highlight of my entire day.

Chapter 21

Devlin had to go out, he was meeting with a client over dinner. Since I wasn't well enough to go with him, he was having Mistress Sophie come by to stay with me. I tried to assure him that I would be fine while he was out for the night, but he wouldn't hear of it. He insisted I have someone over to take care of me in his absence. I'd been feeling much better lately. I was still sore but my bruises had started to fade. Still Devlin was determined to have someone around to take care of me, so what could I do? Plus, I liked spending time with Mistress Sophie again.

I've been seeing a lot of her lately. Her slave was called away for some military assignment overseas so she occupied her free time by taking care of me in the best way she knew how. She was always making sure my room had fresh flowers and most days she spent fixing my hair or moisturizing my skin. Sometimes she would bring her laptop to bed with me and we would shop online together.

"Slave's been gone for a long time now. What's he doing?"

"I don't know," Mistress Sophie said. "He's off playing GI Joe in some God forsaken third world country."

I thought she had said before that he was former Special Forces but that was all I really think she ever mentioned. I didn't realize he was still in the military in some way. Poor Mistress Sophie, she must miss him dearly.

"What exactly does he do in the military? Does he ever talk about it?"

"I don't know. It's all top secret. He can't really say much about it. All I can say for sure it that when he goes on a mission, he is gone for weeks at a time and can't communicate with anyone."

Mistress Sophie took a tiny little phone out of her purse and showed it to me.

"When he lands safely on US soil his friend from command sends me a coded text message, which lets me know that sometime in the next twenty four hours he'll be coming back home to me."

"You must miss him like crazy."

Mistress Sophie waved her hand dismissively in the air. "Don't be ridiculous. I have far more important things to do with my time than to think about slave."

Despite what she might have said, I knew the truth. I could see it in her eyes. She missed her slave and then something else hit me. On the first night I met Mistress Sophie, Devlin she went through slaves like candy. But she'd been with this slave for a while now.

"Mistress Sophie how long have you been with slave?"

"I don't know, a year I suppose -- maybe more. I don't really keep up with those things."

That was a long time. I knew that even if she tried to play causal about their affair, she had deep and real feelings for him.

"What's that cute little pouty lip for?"

"Because Mistress Sophie, every time I try to get to know you better, you just blow me off. I consider you my nearest and dearest friend, like the sister even. I thought you felt the same, but maybe I was wrong."

"No my sweet baby girl. That's so not true." She sighed. "I'm sorry, you're right. I'm not good with sharing things about myself. But for you I'll try. Ask me anything and I'll tell you."

"I want to know about your husband."

"Okay that I wasn't expecting. But I promised, so here goes." Mistress Sophie took a deep breath and began her story.

"I first met my husband to be, Eduardo Rey when I was a skinny, gawky little thirteen year old girl and he was seventeen. It was a brief and rather awkward meeting that our parents arranged. I thought he was so handsome and couldn't wait to grow up and begin my life with him. He clearly didn't feel the same for me. It was easy to see he wasn't happy about our arranged marriage, but that was more than understandable. I was a child with braces and I hadn't quite developed yet."

"When I graduated high school, I was seventeen. I didn't go off to college like my friends. Instead I was sent to South America to be with my husband. I was completely naive to the ways of the world. I spent my entire teenage years dreaming of this perfect husband I would one day marry. I would never even kiss another boy. I wanted to stay perfectly chaste for him in every way."

"My husband however, didn't stay so chaste. He had several relationships before me and even fell madly in love with one particular girl. She had dreams of them getting married but he knew that wouldn't be possible. He knew our families had made the marriage arrangement and there was nothing either of us could do to get out of it."

"Still despite knowing they couldn't ever be married because of me, they pressed on. Not too long before I was due to arrive in South America they went on holiday together during which time they took a hike up a dormant volcano, a popular tourist destination."

"The volcano had been dormant for hundreds of years but on their trek up the mountain, something went wrong. As they reached the summit, they were standing on the ledge of the volcano and went to peer over. The mountain began to shake as an eruptive vent opened up, the girl fell and plummeted two thousand feet into the crater and to her death."

"My husband was devastated at the loss of his beloved, but apparently her family felt it was his fault. They were a deeply spiritual family and they felt this was the girl's punishment from God for sleeping with him when he was already committed to someone else. Her family wouldn't let Eduardo even attend her funeral. He was bitter and angry and then I showed up ready to get married."

"Eduardo hated me for just existing and my life turned into a horrible nightmare as a result. We were married in a small ceremony at his family home in Valencia. We didn't take a honeymoon. Instead I immediately moved into his house where for three months he held me prisoner and repeatedly raped and beat me nearly to death. When people would come visit he would gag me and tie me up in a closet so I would not be seen."

"Oh my goodness. I'm so sorry. How did you break free?"

"After about three months his mother paid us a surprise visit. She found me on the floor nearly dead and rushed me to the hospital. My jaw was broken in three places, my wrist and left ankle were sprained. I had three cracked ribs, and two were broken. I was also severely dehydrated and malnourished."

"Did he not feed you while you were there?"

"He gave me just enough food to keep me alive, but just barely. Each day I would get a glass of water and several pieces of bread and sometimes an apple or a banana."

"What did his family do? Did they know it was him that did that to you?"

"No, not in the beginning. When she first found me since the house was in such a disarray she assumed there was some sort of break in and that some sort of criminal did that to me. I didn't tell the authorities or anyone what had happened at first. I just wanted to go back home to America so I clammed up, fearing that if they knew the truth they might try and shut me up for good."

"My parents flew to see me and hoped that I would speak but still being in a foreign country, I just didn't think it was a good idea to tell anyone the truth. My family took me back to America to recover and his mother came with us. That's when I revealed what happened. I told his mom the whole story and expected her to defend her son but surprisingly she didn't even try. Instead she went to my parents and negotiated a new deal with them."

"I would remain married to Eduardo, even keep his name. I would get a nice lump sum payment up front and a generous monthly allowance. He would live in Venezuela and I would live in Texas."

"Have you seen him since then?"

"No. I get phone calls on occasion from his mother letting me know how he is doing and where he is living now, but until recently I hadn't even heard from him."

"He called you?"

"No, he sent me a letter."

"He wanted to apologize for the troubled time in our marriage and to let me know that he forgives me for any of my infidelities during our union."

"Wait, what? He forgives you? Did he seriously expect you to remain completely loyal and faithful to him after what he did to you?"

"Apparently," Mistress Sophie said sarcastically.

"Why do you think he reached out to you after all of this time? Do you think he wants to reconnect with you?"

"I don't know. I threw the letter away and didn't give it a second thought."

"What if he wants you to get back together?"

"Yeah, it's not going to happen."

"Since you know you two are never going to be together again why don't you just get divorced?"

"It's not an option. His family are devout Catholics and divorce is something they would never allow. They take the sacrament of marriage very serious."

"What if he wants to remarry or you? What if you fall in love are you saying you can never ever marry that person?"

"Not an option. They don't allow divorce under any circumstances."

"There has to be some exception. What about under extreme circumstances like the husband or wife turns out to be a serial killer or rapes babies or something. Seriously even then?"

"You are using logic. You'll find as you get older that logic and religion just don't mix. To them marriage is a union made by God and therefore is unbreakable. When a man and woman commit the rest of their lives to each other, they become one. So if your husband is a serial killer then I guess so are you because you are no longer man and woman, you are one, united under God's endearing light. If he's sick you are sick. If he's unhappy then you are unhappy, because you are now one."

"Okay, seriously you are not all that much older than me."

"I'll have you know, I just turned thirty," Mistress Sophie said with a laugh. "So I have almost an entire decade of experience over you."

If Mistress Sophie couldn't ever divorce her husband then that meant that her relationship with her slave could never really be more than it is right now and that made me feel horribly sad for her. I couldn't imagine what it must be like to be forced to stay married to that monster, which prevented her from ever moving on with her life and truly being with the one she obviously really loved.

"How did you meet your slave?"

"I was attending a charity event and he was there. He was introduced to me as someone in the Army Special Forces, specializing in foreign internal defense. I was impressed with his credentials."

"So that's what first drew you to him?"

"No it was his control. His military training gave him this unbreakable will and I oh so enjoy trying to weaken his resolve."

"He's so big and bad ass looking. I have to admit, I kind of like watching you bend him to your will."

Mistress Sophie laughed.

"Do you think he gets jealous watching the two of us together?"

"Watching us together does drive him crazy. It's one of the few times he seems to lose his ability to focus."

While we were talking Mistress Sophie and I were in my bed and our bodies were intertwined. Hearing her talk about her slave get turned on watching us, got me excited and I started to squirm.

"You naughty little girl," Mistress Sophie chided. "You like the thought of him seeing us together, don't you?"

"Yes," I admitted, embarrassed that it was true. I did like knowing he was watching Mistress Sophie and I together and that it made his dick hard. It's not that I want to be with her slave. I just like knowing that it turns him on to watch us.

Chapter 22

"Did you and Mistress Sophie have a good time tonight?"

I giggled. "Yes, you can say that."

Devlin sat down next to me.

"How about you? Did you have a good time tonight Master?"

"I want to talk to you about something my sweet. Your passport came in the mail today."

"Oh really? I didn't even know that I still had one of those things."

I got my passport when I was in high school. I worked double shifts almost the entire summer to be able to afford to go on the senior trip with my classmates. It wasn't easy coming up with the $3,000 I needed to go but I finally had the money.

That was until two days before we were supposed to leave, my brother got drunk at a party, fell and broke his leg.

We didn't have health insurance and the only money we had to pay the bill was the money from my senior trip. I was devastated. But what could I do? I couldn't not help my brother.

"I renewed it for you a few weeks ago."

"Why Master? Are we going somewhere?"

"Not today, but yes we will be going somewhere that we'll need a passport."

About Veronica Cane

I've been telling stories my whole life. Even as a young child I would delight in sharing them with the other kids in my neighborhood. They were little kids stories about little kid things. As I got older, however my tastes began to change and I found that I most enjoyed writing about love, romance and sexual desire.

I hope that you enjoy reading my stories as much as I loved sharing them with you in the first place. It really is my honor to share my work with you.

If you've enjoyed my work you can join my newsletter so that I can update you about future projects at www.VeronicaCane.com.

Printed in Great Britain
by Amazon